VAMPIRE WITCH IN WESTERHAM

Paranormal Investigation Bureau Book 13

DIONNE LISTER

 Created with Vellum

CHAPTER 1

"Are you ready, Lily?" my sister-in-law, Millicent, asked.

I wiped my sweaty palms on my jean-clad thighs and swallowed. "Yes. I think so."

Will gave me an encouraging smile. "You've got this, Lily. It's not that hard."

I glared at him—he was annoyingly handsome in a tight-ish-fitting long-sleeved black T-shirt and blue jeans. "Easy for you to say. You got this a week ago. Some of us aren't as quick on the uptake." Okay, so frustration was not a good look on me.

"Meow."

I looked down at Abby, who sat on the floor. The long-haired dark-brown-and-white kitty had been part of our family for two weeks, and I still hadn't managed to communicate with her mind to mind. She was so adorable, though, and I couldn't help but smile at what I assumed was her encouragement. My smile fell. Hmm, maybe she was chastising me for being cranky at Will for no good reason. But I wouldn't know because I couldn't read her thoughts. Dammit.

Millicent chuckled. "Lily, stop overthinking it. And Abby was encouraging you…. Don't look at me like that—I didn't read your mind; Abby did."

My forehead tightened. "Don't mind shields work against animals?"

"Only partly. When we think, we project emotions too. Complex thoughts are blocked by mind shields, but our emotions aren't. Half of an animal's understanding, once they can decipher our language, is via picking up on emotions. She's told me you're frustrated—not that I didn't already know. You have no poker face to speak of." I rolled my eyes. She laughed. "Exhibit A."

"You were meant to see that. I was making a statement." I knew I was being ridiculous, but I couldn't help myself. Feeling left out was horrible. What if I could never communicate with Abby and our new dog, Ted? I shut my eyes. Non-witches had totally fulfilling lives with their pets without being able to fully understand them. And these animals had had witch intervention, so they could communicate rather well nonverbally. And if I spoke, they understood me. I opened my eyes. "Okay. I'm fine. Sorry for being cranky. Even if I can't get this stuff, it's not the end of the world. I can still understand them enough to know when they're hungry, happy, or sick, and I can still love them." Abby jumped into my lap and booped her head against my hand. I patted her. *See, Lily. It's not that hard to understand them.* Ted, the previously scruffy dog who had now been groomed into a handsome version of his former self, stood from his spot on the floor next to Will's feet and came over to me, tail wagging. I gave him a firm pat too.

Will smiled. "They love you, and that's all we really need, isn't it?"

I met his warm gaze and smiled back. "Yep. You're right." He smirked. "Well, you have to be right one time out of ten, or it wouldn't be fair." My serene expression was all innocence. He raised a brow.

"Now, now, children." Millicent grinned. "Let's get back to what we were doing. We'll try this one more time, Lily. If you don't get it, don't worry—it will likely come when you least expect it. You're trying too hard. You have to let it happen."

Gah, why was this so confusing? "That's pretty much the opposite of other magic."

She cocked her head to the side. "Yes and no. When you perform normal magic, if it's your talent or something you've done time and time again, you only think about what you want, don't you? It's not a difficult thought process but a simple request. Even with complicated spells, you're concentrating on getting the steps and words right rather than pushing hard with the power itself. You're projecting and straining too much."

"Well, that's so much clearer. Thanks." I shook my head. I didn't think I was straining any harder than I normally did when trying to perfect something I wasn't familiar with. I sighed. Arguing was getting me nowhere. "Okay, one more try, and then I'm done for now."

"Take a deep breath and open your mind up to the room." Millicent's soothing tone was ruined by what she said. I knew just opening my mind wasn't easy, but I'd try, nonetheless.

I shut my eyes and took a deep breath.

I opened my mind.

I waited.

The only things I could sense were my breathing and darkness.

Nothing.

I took a few more breaths. Nope. Not happening. Swallowing the salty rush of defeat, I opened my eyes and pretended I wasn't devastated. "Well, that was a bust." I smiled my fakest of smiles. "Maybe tomorrow."

Millicent's and Will's hopeful faces fell in unison. They weren't buying the snake oil I was selling, but in true kindred fashion, they pretended everything was fine. Millicent shrugged. "Can't win 'em all. But you're right—tomorrow could be the day." She smiled gently, and Abby nudged my hand for another pat. Her soft fur took the sting out of my failure. At least I still had their love.

This time, my smile was genuine—maybe a touch sad, but, hey, I was only human. "It's fine. I'm sure it will happen eventually." Abby purred, and Ted barked once. "At least you guys are making it easy for me." I laughed.

"Squeak, squeak."

I looked at Millicent. Bagel was perched on one shoulder and Cinnamon the other. They twitched their noses at me. A grin spread across my face. "Okay, okay, you're all awesome. Thank you."

Millicent translated their next squeaks. "They said you're welcome, and you shouldn't give up, but even if you never get it, they still love you, flawed human that you are."

My eyes widened, but then I laughed. "You guys are so

honest." At least you got the real deal when you were chatting to animals. From what I could tell from Will's translations at home, Abby tended to put a kinder spin on things when it was all going wrong, and Ted tended to say not much, but they never said anything that wasn't true, and with the rats… well, they were pretty blunt, but I could handle it.

Will stood. "I think we're done here for today. We'll keep working on it at home, Mill."

A baby's cry came from the monitor. "My niece is awake! Can I have a quick cuddle before we go?"

"Of course you can. Why don't you go get her?"

I placed Abby on the couch next to me and jumped up. "Thanks, Mill." I soon returned with a bundle of smiling cuteness. After Will and I both cooed over her and smothered her with kisses, I handed my niece to Millicent.

She took her. "Time for you to have a feed and nappy change." Millicent looked at me, then Will. "Don't forget our meeting tonight at eight."

Will and I shared a serious look. Tonight was all about planning our trip into Dana Piranha's dad's factory. This was going to be dangerous. There was a chance we could get arrested, or worse. And when I say "we," I had no idea who was going in. Chances were that James and Will would make me wait it out since I wasn't an agent. As much as that frustrated me, I understood where they were coming from. Although that didn't mean I was going to let them leave me behind without a fight.

My gut told me that we'd find a huge clue in there, a clue about what had happened to my parents, or at least why they'd been connected to Dana's dad. I refused to believe that my mother was part of the snake group. If she had been, there would've been no reason for them to have killed her and my father. Her seeming friendliness towards them must have been an act.

"Lily?" Will looked at me, his lips twitching up at the corners. "Off with the squirrels again?"

"I can think of worse places to be." I grinned.

"Let's go. Can you take Abby? I'll take Ted." We didn't want them walking through our doorways themselves, just in case they didn't grasp the seriousness of what touching the edges would do.

"Can do." I closed my hands around her soft belly and lifted her to sit against my chest. "You're so warm and squishy."

"Meow."

Millicent laughed. "She said, so are you."

I giggled. "I've been called worse. I'll take that as a win. See you tonight." I smiled at Millicent, then the rats, who'd moved to the couch.

Will and I made our doorways and stepped through to Angelica's. I placed Abby on the floor, opened the reception-room door to a quiet house, and shivered. I furrowed my brow. The quiet wasn't unusual, but there was something *empty* about it. Will came through the door, and I turned to him. "Does it feel weird in here?"

His brows drew down. He looked around, then back down at me, concern on his face. "It's as if something's missing."

"Yes!" I threw up my return to sender. "You don't think someone's breached the protections?" We had several spells protecting the house because being a government agent was never safe, and they'd beefed things up when we'd found out that Regula Pythonissam was after me.

He shook his head. "No, I don't think that's it." He pursed his lips. "When was the last time you saw Angelica?"

"Um…. Four days ago, at dinner. When was the last time you saw her?"

"I saw her that night, then the next day at work. We had a brief meeting on a case Beren and I are working on. I haven't seen her since then." Ted barked. Will looked down at him. "That would be great. Thank you."

"What did he say?" Gah, I hated being in the dark.

"He's offered to help us figure it out. He's going to sniff out her room and tell us when she was last there."

I smiled down at Ted. "Wow, that's impressive!" Ted wagged his tail and looked at me. Just enough of his teeth showed that it looked like he was smiling. "Good boy!"

"Lead the way." Will waited for Ted to start up the stairs, then followed. Abby and I were right behind. Ted sniffed his way to her closed door. Will knocked, and we waited a moment. Getting no answer, he opened it.

While Ted sniffed around her room, and Abby checked things out, Will and I stood in the middle of the space. Nothing seemed out of place—her bed was made, her bedside tables were tidy, window closed, floor vacuumed. It was neatness in a nutshell—typical for Angelica.

"Are you going to check her wardrobe?" I asked. I didn't want to invade her privacy. What if she wasn't gone or missing, and we'd rifled through her things? She would not appreciate it. She was probably on a case somewhere. Maybe I shouldn't have said anything earlier? My radar could be off because I'd failed at talking to the animals. Could disappointment temporarily affect someone's gut instinct?

"I'll wait to see what Ted says. If she was here this morning, there's no reason to."

"So, you don't want to risk invading her privacy either?" I smirked.

"Nope. I don't have a death wish." He winked.

Ted took his time. When he was done, he sat at Will's feet. Will crouched to have a chat. "So, Teddy boy, when was she last here?" Will stared at the dog for a moment, but Ted made no sound. I supposed it was because they spoke to us in visuals and feelings. Whatever Ted was conveying would be directly to Will's brain. I bit my fingernail while I waited for the translation. Will's brow furrowed. Finally, he stood and looked at me. "He's not super clear on the concept of time, but from what he's conveyed, she was last here the morning after the dinner you last saw her. So that would be the day I saw her at work."

"Is she on assignment somewhere?"

"I don't know. I'm not on the list of people who need to know things. I'm going to give your brother a call to meet me. I don't want to do this over the phone." His meaningful look said so much. Could this have something to do with that PIB director wanting her out of the way?

I swallowed the bug of fear scratching my throat. "Um, okay. Let me know what he thinks, will you? I'm worried."

He pulled me into his arms. "It'll be fine. She's a capable witch, Lily. You don't rise to her position in the PIB if you're not. I have to believe she's okay, and until we have proof that she's not, I won't entertain the idea. And I don't want you to either. You've got enough on your plate, and we can't afford distractions." He kissed the top of my head.

"But it's Angelica."

"I know, but she can look after herself. I've worked with her for years, and I've seen how she handles things." He loosened his hold and looked down into my eyes. "Trust me on this. Please?"

I sighed. "Okay, but you know I won't forget about it until we know what's going on. It's just how I am."

He gave me a small smile. "I know, but I have to at least try. But, honestly, if I thought she was in huge trouble right now, I'd be doing everything I could to find her. Let's just see what happens. Okay?"

I blew out a forceful breath. "Okay." A squishy weight pressed against my leg. I looked down. Abby rubbed her body against my leg and looked up. "You're such a cutie, and I can't resist." I bent and picked her up, then cuddled her to my chest, her front paws resting on my shoulder. "Such a gorgeous kitty."

Will stroked her head, then scratched under her chin, eliciting a purr. Then his phone rang, ruining our family moment. And, yes, fur kids were family. They'd only been in our lives for a couple of weeks, but I didn't know how we'd lived without them for so long.

"Hey, James…. Yes, coming in now. Yep…. Ah, good. See you soon." He hung up.

"So?"

"James needs to see me about a case he's been working on, so I'll talk to him then. I might not be home for dinner tonight. I'll probably just meet you at James's at eight."

I pouted, all the disappointment going straight to my lips. Was it weird that it did that? With Angelica MIA, it would only be me… eating alone. Abby meowed, and Ted barked. I shook my head and laughed. "You're both right—I won't be alone. I've got you guys." Abby licked my cheek. It was like having my face sanded, but it was still cute. "Keep me updated, please."

"I probably won't be able to tell you anything till I see you later. You never know who's listening in." He gave me a quick kiss on the lips before his work uniform replaced his normal clothes. "See you tonight."

"Bye."

He made his doorway and left. I hugged Abby tighter. Looked like these guys had arrived just in time to save me from myself. "Why don't we go have some lunch and watch TV?" Abby wriggled in my arms, indicating she wanted to get down, so I placed her on the floor, and they both followed me to the kitchen.

I magicked myself a cheese-and-tomato toastie and grabbed a bit of cooked chicken for my little companions. I placed their food in their respective bowls—Abby's was a ceramic bowl that said Boss Lady, and Ted's said Top Dog. Abby didn't mind the top-dog thing. She'd said—according to Will's translation—that since she wasn't a dog, it was fine.

I settled myself on the couch in the TV room. Phone next to me and plate on my lap, I used the remote to turn the TV on. Ah, the news. I wasn't quite sure if that's what I felt like watching. Before I could change the channel, Ted ran in, followed by Abby, who looked to be chasing him. Ted stopped abruptly and turned to face Abby, his front legs stretched out in front, bum in the air, tail straight up—a common display I'd seen before, which I thought meant play with me more. Abby sat and booped Ted gently on the nose. The whole thing was so adorable that I had to pick up my phone and take a picture.

I snapped off a few because they were still playing, but then I noticed something and stopped. Huh? I stared at the TV, then compared that to what was on my phone camera. The reporter on the news was in a street in Westerham, in the daylight, talking about someone who was suing council over an uneven footpath, which they tripped on and broke their arm. That wasn't the important part though. In my photo, lying on the ground on the front steps of a church behind the reporter was a woman. Standing over her was a tall man, his back to me. It was night, but a porch light on the church lit the scene enough for me to tell what it was. When I looked at the TV, they weren't there, and it was day again. The segment finished, and we were back with the news presenter in the studio.

Well, that had never happened before. Just when I thought my magic couldn't surprise me, it shows me a crime via the television. I stared down at the photo on my phone and made it bigger, focussing on the woman on the ground. Her eyes were closed, her body limp. Was she dead or just unconscious? Goosebumps slithered along my arms, and I shuddered. Surely she was dead? My magic didn't normally step in for no reason. I sighed, my sandwich no longer the temptation it was two minutes ago. There was nothing like a potentially dead body to quieten the hunger pangs. And who was that man? Had he stopped to check on her, or had he killed her?

I called James.

"Hey, Lily. I'm just busy at the moment. Can it wait?"

"Um, I was hoping I could come in and talk to you. It might be able to wait, but I'm not sure." Who knew? Maybe this crime—provided it was one—had happened two years ago. There was no way for me to tell. It wasn't like my talent gave me a time and date neatly stamped in the corner of the photo. "I can't really explain over the phone."

"Okay. I get it. I'll have about ten minutes in an hour. Come by the office then."

"Thanks. See you later."

I did some googling about female murders in the area in the last two years, and I found nothing about a woman's body being found on the front porch of a church. There were four articles on missing women. Unfortunately, the photo I'd taken was too far away and grainy for any facial particulars to stand out enough that I could match any of those pictures to her. What had the news person said? Hosey Hill. There couldn't be too many churches on that street. Although it was the UK— there were churches all over the place, so maybe we'd have a few to choose from. If worst came to worst, I was sure we could find a copy of that news report and watch it.

After practically counting the minutes till I could leave, an hour had passed. I bade farewell to the fur babies and made a doorway to PIB headquarters. Surprisingly, Gus didn't answer the door. I was almost disappointed—that is to say, I would've been disappointed, except the guy who answered the door was drop-dead gorgeous. And, don't worry—I hadn't forgotten Will, but, as they say, I wasn't blind. To be honest, he reminded me a little of Will. He had the same thick, dark hair, but where Will's eyes were stormy grey-blue, this guy's were brilliant blue, and he had thick, dark lashes women would pay for—pay for the lashes, that is, not the man.

"State your name and reason for your visit." His demeanour was all businesslike, but there was a slight twinkle in his eyes. Or was that my imagination?

"Lily Bianchi. I'm here to see Agent Bianchi."

"Are you his wife?"

"No. Sister."

A small smile turned his lips up. "Have you got ID?"

"Um, no. I don't normally need it." That was stupid on my part… and what else was new? I had ID at home. "I can go get it."

"You do that."

Okay, then. He was a stickler for the rules. I sighed as he shut the door. Then I magicked my ID to me. I mean, I could've done that with the door open, but since unapproved people couldn't magic things to themselves in the building, he probably thought I'd have to go home. I buzzed the door again. He opened it. "Back so soon?"

I waved my ID in front of me. "I have clearance to magic things." I used my second sight. He was a witch, too, which made him more dangerous than Gus, who was a non-witch. Were they beefing up security, or was I just being paranoid?

This time, he grinned. "Well, come in, then. Sorry to make you go through that, but we can't be too careful. Do you need an escort?"

I smiled. "No thanks. I know my way around."

"Well, if you need anything… anything at all, let me know." His cute grin showed off straight, white teeth. He really was the whole package. I stifled a giggle because there probably were people who had that on their list of partner must-haves. As long as someone had teeth, well, I'd be happy with that.

"Thanks. I'll be sure to let you know." I gave him a small wave and hurried to James's office. He didn't have much time to speak to me, and New Guy had just wasted two minutes of it. And as for asking him for help with anything—I had Will. I grinned. Ah, Will. Yeah, I still hadn't stopped sighing over him. He made me feel like the luckiest woman ever.

When I reached James's door, I knocked but went straight in, not bothering to wait for an answer. He had a receptionist today. I stopped dead, my mouth hanging open. I might have even blinked several times. "Gus? What are you doing here?"

He winked. "I'm learning the ropes. Agent Bianchi needs a full-time assistant, and I'm not getting any younger, so I thought I'd go for it. I've been doing some online typing classes. Liv's been teaching me the ins and outs of the computer system, and I've even practiced my phone manner." He lifted an imaginary phone to his ear. "Good morning, Agent Bianchi's office. How may I help you?"

I chuckled. "That's awesome! Well, congrats on the job change. I was wondering why there was a new guy at the reception room."

"Ah, Tommy. He started a few days ago. They've been moving him around, getting him familiar with everything."

James appeared at his office door. "Lily? Why are you yammering here? I haven't got much time left." His annoyed-brother face was not my most favourite.

"Oops, sorry. Chat later, Gus." I followed James in. He didn't bother sitting—he stood next to his table with his arms folded. I made a bubble of silence, then handed him my phone, one of the pictures from this morning on the screen. "Check that out."

He grabbed my phone and looked. His brow wrinkled as he squinted and enlarged the picture. "Is that what I think it is?"

"If you're talking about the woman lying on the porch and the guy standing over her, then, yes, it is. I can't tell if she's dead or unconscious, but whatever it is, it wasn't on TV. It only came through when I was taking a picture of Ted and Abby playing."

"This isn't much to go on, Lily. I think your next step is to go out there and actually take some photos. We'll need a clearer picture of her face, and maybe you can get his face too? Then we can at least try and match hers to missing persons. If she turns up, we'll have a lead." He handed my phone back.

"It's in Westerham, so I'll probably drive, but with RP out there, I'll need someone to go with me. Even two someones would be good."

"Will and Imani?"

"Sounds good to me. When can you spare them?"

"Not today, I'm afraid." He rubbed his chin. "I don't want to leave it too long, though. What if it is a crime and it's recent? Then we'll be slow starting the investigation, and evidence could be lost." He looked at the ceiling and huffed out a breath. "Tomorrow morning, early. I'll send Imani over at seven. Who knows, you might even get the jump on RP if they're napping in their van."

"Yeah, ha ha. They haven't been that obvious for a while. I

hope they're freezing cold hiding behind a bush somewhere. That would serve them right."

James laughed. "Nice. That would be part of an apt punishment." He slipped his phone out of his pocket and checked it. "I have to get going. Sorry. Busy day."

I removed the bubble of silence. "It's fine. I understand." Story of my life, understanding. But I couldn't complain. I had the best friends and family. It would be greedy of me to ask for more. "Stay safe. Oh, and nice secretary." I chuckled. "Gus is awesome. Just don't ask him about his dog."

Gus appeared at the door. "Did I hear my name mentioned?"

"Yes. I was just telling James that you have a habit of talking about your dog."

His brow furrowed. "What's wrong with that?"

"Well, nothing, really, if you leave out the stories with poo and vomit." Okay, so I'd finally said it. It was time someone did.

"Oh, do those topics bother you, Miss Lily?" His face was slack with worry.

"If I'm honest? Yes. Sorry. I didn't know how to tell you."

Gus smiled. "Not a problem. I'll make sure to leave those things out. As long as I can still talk about my gorgeous boy, I'm happy."

"Excellent." I gave him a huge smile. "And now James has to leave, so I'm going to get going too. See you both later." Feeling slightly guilty about my admission, but not guilty enough that I wanted to take it back, I made my doorway and left. Hopefully now my conversations with Gus would always be pleasant.

What wasn't pleasant was the meeting tonight and the fact that Angelica was potentially missing. Both things were important and scary, and I had no idea how we'd deal with either of them. We'd been fairly lucky up till now, getting to the bottom of different things and surviving. But I had a horrible feeling our luck was about to run out.

CHAPTER 2

8:10 p.m. and I sat between Liv and Imani at my brother's dining-room table, Bagel on my shoulder. Will and James still hadn't arrived. Millicent sat opposite me, and Beren sat to her left. Millicent tapped the table with the fingers of one hand. "Don't worry, Lily. They've just been flat out today. Ma'am's taken leave, and Chad fired another agent, but they're not putting anyone else on."

If Ma'am had taken leave, where was she? Surely she hadn't gone on holidays and not told us. "Bloody hell. Who did he fire?" I hoped it wasn't someone I liked.

Beren frowned. "Agent Cardinal."

My shoulders sagged. "Oh. He wasn't my favourite person, but he was trustworthy and on Ma'am's side." I gazed at Beren, then Millicent. "You don't think they're going to get rid of you guys, too, do you?"

Millicent shook her head. "No, I don't think so. It's just budget cuts."

Beren didn't look so sure. "Who knows. But we can't worry about that now. There's nothing we can do about it even if that's what's happening. And, to be honest, I don't think it is. Let's wait and see how many people lose their jobs over the next six months, and if the ratio of Ma'am supporters to those who are neutral or don't like her are out of whack, we'll consider it then."

Voices floated in from the hallway. I smiled despite our less-than-positive conversation. Will and James must have arrived. I stood and placed Bagel on the table, then snorted because it rhymed. Will and James came into the room.

"It's about time!" I pushed my chair out and hurried to Will to give him a big smooch and hug.

He slid his hand under my hair and rested his warm palm on the back of my neck. "Well, hello, gorgeous. Why don't I get this kind of greeting every day?"

"What are you talking about? You do most days, but I was worried when you guys were late. Is everything okay?"

He shrugged. "Pretty much. Just flat out."

"Yep. Flat out like a lizard drinking." James bent to give Millicent a quick kiss, then took his place at the head of the table as I sat back down, and Will sat at the foot of the table.

"Flat out like a what?" Beren asked.

"Like a lizard drinking." James laughed. "It's an Aussie saying, mate." He winked. "It means we were really busy."

"Yeah, yeah, I got that bit. But it has to be said—you Aussies are a weird breed."

James and I shared a smile and a nod. I turned to Beren. "Yes, but you Brits wouldn't have it any other way, would you?"

Beren laughed. "Yeah, okay, you got me."

James magicked a coffee onto the table in front of him. "Does anyone want tea or coffee?" Everyone murmured that they were good. "Okay, then. Time to get to it. Now, Millicent and I have done some planning based on what we learned from the rats' warehouse mission and what I know everyone's skills are." He clasped his hands in front of him on the table, then looked directly at me. "I don't want any arguments about the choices I've made. Is that clear?"

I blinked, being between and rock and a hard place. If I answered that it was clear, the assumption was that I wouldn't argue, and James knew when someone lied. I gave him a cheesy smile.

"That's not an answer, Lily." He gave me his stern-dad face.

"Would you like me to lie to you?"

"No. I would like you to agree with me. Just once, can you make things easier? Please?" His eyes implored me to not insist on going in. It wasn't because he didn't think I could handle it, but he was worried something would happen to me. Even knowing this, it rankled.

I sighed. "Okay. But I'm going on record as saying that I hate being left out again. I'm going to be worried about whoever goes in there, and it's our fight, James, not anyone else's."

Imani cleared her throat. "Your sentiment is worthy, love, but I beg to differ. This is everyone's fight now. Even though RP are after you and had something to do with your parents' disappearance, they've hurt many other people in order to further their agenda, whatever it might be. The only reason the PIB isn't going after them is that Ma'am doesn't trust everyone in there, and once RP knows for sure the PIB are going hard for them, they'll up their game, and it will be all-out war. I, for one, don't want to go into war with enemies in our midst. RP are dangerous to the whole world and have to be stopped. It just so happens that we're the little group who have to do it." She rested her hand on my arm in a soothing gesture. "Don't worry—you'll get your chance on the front lines. This just isn't that moment. Let us do our jobs, and later, you can do yours. We all have a part to play."

"Why do you have to be so damn sensible?" How could I argue with Imani's logic? She was right, and I'd be an idiot to argue—not that me realising I was doing something idiotic was normally a deterrent….

"So, we're good?" James asked.

"Yeah. Peachy." Okay, so my unhappy expression didn't quite match what I was saying, but it was official: I'd given up, and James knew it.

"Thanks, Lily. Trust me when I say that we'll all do our jobs better knowing you're safe." He gave a small smile, then refocussed on everyone else at the table. "Right, so how are we going to pull this off? The factory has major security—cameras, magic, and guards. There is one area in particular we're aiming for, and that's the basement via the trapdoor the rats found last time. We're hoping to find paperwork and possibly something else that will incriminate them—drugs, weapons, illegal magical items, those kinds of things. If we can't find anything incriminating and we get caught, not only will we lose our jobs, we'll likely go to jail."

Oh, crap. I hadn't thought of that. I shook my head. Of

course I hadn't. Typical of me to not realise something because it didn't apply to me. My face contorted into several different weirdnesses. The urge to speak was as bad as my need to go to the toilet at that rich guy's place last month. "Gah!" Oops, that came out a little louder than I wanted it to. Everyone turned to stare at me, James's expression conveying *I can't believe you're going to argue when you promised you wouldn't.* "I don't want to argue, but I just want to point out that out of everyone here, I'm the only one who has nothing to lose job wise. You can't all risk yourselves like this. Where will we be without all your PIB resources? Worse still, what the hell will happen if you all go to jail?" I shook my head. "This is just too much."

Liv nodded. "As much as I love Lily and don't want anything to happen to her, what she says makes total sense. I also know how strong she is in the power department. I vote that she's one of the ones to go in." I turned and smiled at my best friend. She got it. When all was said and done, it was better to risk someone with nothing to lose.

"And I don't have kids. James, you and Millicent can't afford to go to jail. You can't do that to Annabelle." I had to say it even though there was no way it would be appreciated. It was a fact, and a huge one.

James pressed his lips together. "Look, Lily, you don't think Mill and I haven't discussed this in detail? You haven't heard the plan yet. Why don't you save your worry until you hear what I'm proposing?"

"Fine, but if I don't like it, I can't stay silent." James raised one brow, as if to say, then why did you promise? To be honest, I'd had the best of intentions, but things changed.

James huffed. "Right, can I get on with this, then?" I nodded. "Gee, thanks. Anyway, as I was saying… it's crucial we get through this undiscovered. I'd like everyone's thoughts on this. If you disagree"—he turned to eyeball me, and I folded my arms—"except if your name is Lily Bianchi, please let me know your thoughts. This is still a rough plan, and I'm open to changing it."

"Sounds good to me." Will's gaze when he looked at me was as stern as they came. He was likely ensuring I knew he was on my brother's side with this. Well, of course he was. He loved me and didn't want me in harm's way. I got it—I really did—but I was just as capable of worrying about everyone else as they were of worrying about me.

"No complaints here," said Imani.

"All good." Gah, even Beren was against me. Traitors. Liv patted my arm, and I sad-pouted and nodded. Then Bagel scurried up my arm and sat on my shoulder. She nuzzled into my neck. At least two someones were on my side. I smiled and whispered, "Thanks, ladies."

James cleared his throat. "Okay, back to it. Our plan is this: Because we have Annabelle, Millicent will stay home and monitor from here. There's no use both of us getting involved on-site. Apart from being unnecessary, it's obviously danger-ous." He gazed at Beren. "For a start, you and I are going to knock out both guards." Beren's only reaction was to blink a couple of times. "Yes, I know. It's not going to be easy. But they'll have return to senders up, which won't disappear until we render them unconscious. Also, because we don't want to leave any evidence behind, we're going to have to trap them somewhere without casting a spell on them."

Yikes. This was getting more complicated by the second. How were they supposed to do that? If they used their handcuffs and a cage, unless they could keep them unconscious, someone would guess it was an attack from the PIB, or at least from some kind of witch law enforcement, and I wasn't sure there were any others around.

"How are we going to do that?" asked Beren.

"After we render them unconscious, we'll administer propofol, which will knock them out. I'm counting on your medical expertise to get this right—we don't want to accidentally kill them. I've managed to get the medical history on their guards, just to make sure giving them this drug won't kill them. Four of their guards are in good health and don't have any allergies or other medication. We've been scoping the place out since last time we were there, and they tend to work the same shifts in the same pairings. Based on that information, we'll hit the factory in four nights, when we estimate Alphonso Pucci and Brandon Clements are on. If we get there and they're not on, we'll abort and reschedule. I don't want any surprises."

"Fair call." Beren nodded. "I can easily get what we need, but I'd prefer to have them somewhere other than on the ground while I'm monitoring them. Can we move them into a van while we're waiting?"

"Yes, for sure."

Will gave a quick low wave, grabbing James's attention. "And what's happening with their security cameras while all this is going on? I would imagine you don't want any of this recorded."

James smiled. "You would imagine right. I was hoping you

could come up with something since you handled them last time. The external video feed is the same as the internal one?"

"Yes. Can you get a drone there to record the guards making their rounds? If you can get it at a similar angle to what the cameras have it, I can refeed those images so they're not just getting empty spaces. Covering the inside of the warehouse was easier—it doesn't take much to loop the image of a dark, empty room or freeze things, but if things are being monitored from somewhere else, they'll wonder where their guards have gone."

James nodded at Will. "Good point. I knew you'd have an answer. That puts us at the factory in five days, then. I'll get those images next time Pucci and Clements are there, and then we'll have to hope the weather doesn't change." He ran a hand through his hair. "So many moving parts to this."

Imani shrugged. "Not to worry, love. We'll just take it as it comes. If we have to postpone, we have to postpone. It's not a big deal. Safety needs to be our number-one priority."

Millicent nodded. "Agreed."

James gave a resigned smile. "I know, and it's all good. It's not like I haven't helped Angelica put scores of these missions together, but this is… personal. And the people I'm sending in there, well, I can't afford to lose any of them. Which brings me around to who I'd like to send in." James looked at me, apology in his eyes. Then he turned to Will. "I'd like you to accompany Imani." He looked at Imani, as if to get her approval.

She smiled. "I'm in." She turned to me. "Don't you worry, Lily. Will and I are going to be in and out with no fuss. We'll find what we need and get out of there."

I gave her a brittle smile—if anything happened to her or Will, I'd never live with myself. "That's all well and good, Imani, but how the hell are you supposed to get in there?"

My brother cleared his throat. "Listen closely. This is my plan."

In five days, everything could change, and not for the better.

I loved my brother, and he was a hell of an agent, but I didn't like this.

Not one. Little. Bit.

CHAPTER 3

7:05 a.m. Imani, Will, and I stood behind a church in the early spring chill after having travelled here. Instead of driving, Imani had made a landing spot for us to travel to. At least RP wouldn't bother us. I still had my return to sender up though. You never knew when trouble would strike.

I shivered, snuggled deeper into my black coat, and yawned. Even the cold wasn't enough to wake me up after a night of tossing and turning and trying to stop manic thoughts bouncing around my brain. Will nudged me with his elbow. "Wake up, princess. You've got work to do."

Imani grinned. "You're such a sleepyhead in the mornings, love. Is it an Aussie thing?"

"I won't insult all the Aussies and say yes. It's a wonderfully unique trait all my own." I stuck my tongue out and immediately regretted it. Man, it was cold.

"Ah, we got the bum Aussie, then. Fair enough." Cheeky

woman. She looked at Will. "I'll check around here and the car park for magic signatures. You can check the front while Lily does her thing."

"Sounds good." He linked his arm through mine and half dragged me towards the front of the church. I took little shuffling footsteps—my stiff legs weren't capable of much more. "Don't worry, legs," I whispered, "I hear you. We'll spend the rest of the day in front of the fire after this. I promise."

Will chuckled. "You certainly are wonderfully unique. I don't think I've heard anyone talk to their own legs before."

"Have you heard them talking to other people's legs, then?"

His forehead wrinkled. "No. What?"

"Never mind. I just thought…."

"Mmmhmm." He laughed. "Okay, here we are. The front porch of the church. Pass me your phone?" I reluctantly took it out of my pocket, exposing my hand to the frigid air. Will checked out the photo I'd taken from the television and compared it to the front of the church. "It's definitely the same place." He handed my phone back. I switched it to camera mode and walked a few paces from the church so I could get a general shot to begin.

A jogger with earbuds in ran past, down the hill, not giving us a second glance. I watched him until I was sure he wasn't from RP and going to come back and attack. "Lily?" Will came and stood next to me. "What's wrong?"

"Um, nothing. I'm just a bit jittery, I guess. Just making sure no one's going to sneak up on us."

He stood in front of me, gripped my upper arms, and stared into my eyes. "We're safe right now. Okay? Why don't you take the photos while I keep watch, and when you're done, you can keep watch, and I'll look for a magic signature?"

The aggravation to my nerves diminished somewhat. "You're so good to me. Thanks."

He kissed the top of my head. "I love you. I want you to feel safe…. Hell, I want you to *be* safe. Anyway, let's get this done. Imani and I have to go into headquarters early today."

"Okay, boss."

He grinned. He loved it when I called him boss.

"I love it when you call me boss."

I laughed and nodded. "I know." I squeezed his cheeks affectionately with one hand, making his lips pucker like a surprised fish, and then I turned and unlocked my phone again. Time to point and shoot. "Show me the woman on the ground I saw on the TV." The picture through my phone went dark.

Showtime.

A faint halo of light domed the porch, framing the silhouette of a man. Now the Queen song came into my brain. What the hell was wrong with me today? I shook my head. *Concentrate.* Maybe this was what happened when I was expected to work before I'd had coffee or food. I was surprised my talent cooperated. Before I forgot why I was here, I snapped off a shot. The woman's dark shape wasn't going to tell me much, so I made my way to the porch.

Of course the guy was wearing a wide-brimmed hat pulled low, to his eyebrows, and the light wasn't hitting his face. He also had a neck warmer covering his lips. I had to angle my camera up because he was taller than me. The only feature I could grab was his straightish nose, and even that would be hard to pick out of a line-up.

I'd taken all the photos of him that I needed, so I crouched down and tried to get a picture of her face, but she was lying on her stomach, her head turned to the side. It was really dark where she was, but I managed a side profile image. Not super clear, but maybe clear enough to match it with any photos on a police file—not that we could show anyone this, or they'd think we'd killed her. If she was even dead. Her eyes were closed, so I couldn't tell. I squinted. Her hair had fallen to the side, revealing what seemed to be two small bruises on the side of her neck, or at least tiny circles.

Her earlobe wasn't right either. It was hard to tell—the lack of light washed out all colour—but her earlobe looked ripped, like an earring had been yanked out. I assumed the black coating on it was blood. *Click, click.*

I stood and went to Will, who was dutifully still keeping an eye out. "What've you got?"

"Check this out." I handed him the phone, then eyeballed the street—no one was going to creep up on me.

Something touched my shoulder, and I screamed and turned around faster than a mother who's just told her kid off, is walking away, and hears an under-breath mumble. Okay, so I needed eyes in the back of my head.

A laughing Imani greeted me. "You should've seen your face."

"Damn you, woman! Don't do that! Who cares about RP when my friends can just give me a heart attack and do me in?"

Imani's grin was clear evidence that she didn't care. My

poor heart was still racing. Did that mean I'd done my cardio for the day?

"Check this out." Will handed Imani my phone, then turned to me. "I'm going to check for magic signatures, and there's something else I might find if we're lucky."

Colour me intrigued. "What?"

"I wouldn't want to ruin the surprise, especially if I don't find anything." Before I could say anymore, he'd turned and was making his way to the porch.

Imani handed my phone back. "Wow, love. That doesn't look good."

"Do you reckon she's dead? I found it hard to tell."

She shrugged. "I have no idea, but to be honest, I'd say she's a goner. That rip in her ear would've hurt like hell. Unless she's ridiculously drunk or drugged, she'd be in immense pain, which would wake her up."

"Oh, crap. What do you think the guy is doing?"

"He's either a concerned passer-by or the perp. We'll know soon enough. If we can track her down to a police report, we'll know who called it in, or how she was discovered. If it was the priest who works here or someone else coming to the church, we can assume this guy likely had something to do with it."

"What if we don't find a record of it?"

"We can assume that maybe she was out of it, and this guy got her home safely? I don't know at this stage. For what it's worth, I didn't find any magic signatures. And you have to consider that this could've happened a year or two ago, or even longer."

"Right." Well, all of that was depressing. What if she was fine, but we never figured out who she was, so we never knew she was okay? If that was the case, I'd have to let it go eventually. How long that would take was anyone's guess. But then why would my magic show her to me? "What if that guy killed her, then buried her somewhere?"

She shook her head. "I don't know, Lily. Let's not get ahead of ourselves. We're doing our initial due diligence right now. Patience, love."

I sighed. Story of my life. Thankfully, Will returned, a smile indicating he might just have found something. I cocked my head to the side. "Spill."

He held up a plastic bag. "I think I've found our victim's earring."

I blinked. Imani nodded and said, "Impressive. That has to be a world record for finding evidence. Can I have a look?" She reached out and took the bag, scrutinising its contents through the clear plastic.

I let her have a decent look, then held my hand out. "My turn." She passed it over. A silver flower, its layers of tiny petals viewed as if from the top, dangled from a little hook. Specks of what looked like dirt wedged in between the petals, or maybe it was blood? I swallowed, imagining the pain of having this ripped through my ear. Was this the clue we needed to figure this out?

Will took the bag back and slid it in his inside jacket pocket. "We can't be sure it's hers, of course, but I would say it's unlikely someone else dropped it in just that spot. We might have some luck tracking this woman down. I'll get it to forensics this morning. I didn't find any magical remnants, though. This crime might be a few weeks or months old."

"Right, time to go, then, loves. See you, Lily." Imani gave

me a quick hug, then made her way behind the church to create her doorway. Even though we had no-notice spells activated, someone still might see her—the weirdness of a disappearing person could be hard to ignore.

Will and I followed her, giving each other a kiss before making our doorways and leaving. After the freezing start to the morning, I was looking forward to spending the day in front of the fire reading, but, as usual, the universe had absolutely no respect for my expectations. Wow, what a surprise.

CHAPTER 4

I'd just finished my third cup of coffee, so why was I still yawning? Getting up so early made eleven in the morning feel like four in the afternoon. I absently stroked Abby's head—she was snuggled on my lap in the armchair in front of the fire. Shutting my iPad case, I yawned again. Seriously? At this point, I'd have to have a nap. I was entering my twilight years too early.

My phone rang, and I started. Well, that was one way to wake up. Imani's name appeared on the screen. "Hey, chicky. Miss me already?"

"No, not really."

"Argh, how you wound me."

She laughed. "You're such a nutter. I called because I need to come over. Are you at home?"

"Where else would I be? Everyone I know works, and since I'm not allowed to go anywhere by myself…."

"Yeah, yeah, I'm playing the world's tiniest violin. See you in a jiff." If I was ever looking for sympathy for not much, I definitely wasn't going to get it from Imani. She didn't let me get away with anything. Which was kind of nice. Holding your own pity party could get out of hand if you didn't have take-no-crap friends to help you get out of it.

I stood and gently transferred Abby to the chair, then made my way to the door. Imani's knock sounded as I reached the hall. "Who is it?" The intercom showed it was Imani, but it was fun to mess with her.

"It's me—your favourite friend."

"That's debatable." I opened the door and smirked. "Please come in."

She smiled. "I thought you'd never ask." She walked through to the living room. I locked the door and joined her on one of the Chesterfields. "How come you've got the fire going? It's not cold."

My eyes widened. "You've got to be kidding me. It's thirteen degrees today. Not cold?"

She waved her hand. "Pfft. You Aussies are so soft."

My mouth dropped open. Where was my retort? Dammit, brain! Where's your smarty-pants comment when I need it? I'd failed myself again. Tonight, at about 11:00 p.m., when I was about to drop off to sleep, the perfect comeback would pop into my head. I just knew it. Wasn't that always the way? In my next life, I wanted to reincarnate as someone who always had the perfect response in any situation.

"Lily? Hello, is anybody in there?" She waved her hand in front of my face.

"Oh, sorry. Your whole insulting-me thing was boring, so I

tuned out." Yes! I fist-pumped the air. There it was—my perfect response. I grinned.

Imani laughed. "Doesn't take much to amuse you, does it?"

"Nope."

"Great. Now that's settled, I have lots to tell you." Even though our house was protected by various powerful wards, Imani created a bubble of silence. It was a good habit to be in.

I sat up straighter, eager to find out the details. "Why couldn't you tell me over the phone or at the PIB?"

She looked at me as if to say *You're kidding, right?* "How did we find out about this potential crime?"

My cheeks heated. "Oh, yeah, that." My talent needed to stay a secret at all costs—I had enough people after me as it was.

"Yes, *that*. Anyway, we got Liv to look up missing women in the system—not a weird request that would draw attention, and since she works for James and Millicent, she's asked to research a lot of cases related to different agents. It's a good thing James manages many cases. Chad likes to think he's got his finger on the pulse, but he's got no idea." She shook her head.

"So what did Liv find out?" Hopefully she discovered that nothing had happened. I sighed—I wasn't naïve enough to believe that. The fact that my talent showed me something meant that a crime had been committed. There was no getting around it.

"We found records of a witch who we think is a good match for your lady. Twenty-two-year-old Lana Phillips. Her parents reported her missing just over six months ago after she didn't return home from a Magic Spark date."

"Huh? Magic Spark? Is that a dating site for witches?"

"Yep."

"Oh my God! How did I not know this? What else is everyone not telling me about? I swear, new witches should get a handbook or something." The more I found out it seemed the less I knew. My awakening only highlighted my ignorance.

"Don't stress. You know a lot of what you need to. It's not a biggie."

Of course it wasn't, at least not when you compared it to being murdered, which is likely what'd happened to Lana Phillips. I was getting distracted. How unusual. "Sorry. What else did you find out?"

"Well, your photo wasn't super clear, but from the photo we had on file, it appears to be her. Will's looked up her social media, and he found a picture of her wearing those rose earrings."

I sucked in a breath. "Oh, wow." That was good news, but also not good news. That poor girl was missing. "What about DNA? Did Will get forensics to test the earring?"

"No."

"No?!"

"Until we can explain how he came by that earring, we can't alert anyone. I do have a friend—a non-witch one—who works for the police. I'm going to get her to take a look at it for us. Lana's details will be in their system too since it's an open case, but my lady can do this under the table, so to speak."

As if finding the answers to a missing person's case wasn't

complicated enough, we had to be all hush, hush. "So now what? We wait?"

"Yes, and no. Liv is looking to see if there are any other missing-persons cases we need to check out. We're bound to come across something that we can explain without bringing your photos into it. Until then, we'll have to keep a low profile on this one."

"Just great. And in the meantime, there could be a killer out there somewhere?"

Imani's concerned face said it all. "Yep." She stood. "If we need any more photos, I'll let you know, but for now, sit tight. We're going through all the files on the case—the interviews with her parents and friends, and her phone records from that night. We'll do what we can to accidentally happen upon the case, if you know what I mean. Then we can take it to Chad and get him to okay an investigation."

I stood. "The sooner you guys can do that, the better."

"Yeah, I know. Anyway, enjoy the rest of your day in front of the fire, Aussie softie."

I laughed. "I will, you old English boot."

She snorted. "What the?"

"Well, an old leather boot wouldn't feel the cold." I shrugged.

"You couldn't come up with something else, like a polar bear, or a statue, or something?"

"It was the first thing that popped into my head. Go figure?" I shrugged, and for once, I managed not to smile. Maybe there was hope for my poker face yet. "Make sure you let me know if you find anything."

"Will do, love." She gave me a quick hug, made her doorway, and went back to work, leaving me with a sense of uneasiness and frustration.

As soon as I sat down again, Abby jumped onto my lap. I stroked her back as she padded in a circle, looking for the most comfortable position, her soft fur a pleasant distraction. "Thanks, missy. You're a sweetie. You knew I needed a cuddle." She purred loudly, the soothing rumble settling my nerves. "How did I manage to live without a cat all this time? I'm so glad you've come into my life, Abby." I smiled down at her. She purred even louder, and for a few glorious minutes, I lived in the here and now. I was lucky to have everything I did. In this moment, I was safe, warm, and happy, and I was going to enjoy every last second.

"Lily." Someone stroked my cheek. "Lily, wake up."

"Huh?" I opened my eyes. I'd obviously been enjoying my time with Abby so much that I'd lain on the Chesterfield and fallen asleep. Abby, who was cuddled into my stomach, stretched out, her paws doing their adorable starfish impersonations. I wiped the drool off the side of my mouth with the back of my sleeve, sat up groggily and acknowledged Will. "What are you doing here?" I sat straighter, my eyes wide. "Oh my God. Is it night-time already? Did I sleep through the whole day?" I jerked my head around to look at the window. Adrenaline pumped through my body, shocking me into being wide awake. Not my preferred way to come to my senses.

Will laughed. "No. It's just gone three in the afternoon."

I sucked in a huge relieved breath. It was gloomy outside,

but it wasn't middle-of-the-night dark. "Thank goodness. I only meant to have a quick cuddle with Abby. I'm not sure what happened."

Will smirked. "We made you get up too early, apparently."

"You're right. It's all your fault, and Imani's." Will sat next to me and grabbed Abby for a hug. "You're going to get fur all over your suit." That was the only negative to having animals that I'd discovered—fur everywhere.

He looked at me like I was a simpleton. "Right, because I can't magic it away?"

I bit my bottom lip. "Oh, yeah, that. I forgot. Anyway, enough about me. Why are you home so early?"

His face took on its distinct work position. Damn. "We've unearthed a missing-person's case from three weeks ago. Another young woman—a witch—who'd gone out with friends. She didn't live far from the nightclub they'd gone to and walked home, but she never got there. She lives by herself, so no one raised the alarm until the next afternoon. We've checked street video of that night, and she makes it halfway home; then we're out of video recordings. She's gone missing somewhere between halfway home and home, so at least we have a roughly one-mile stretch to work with."

"That's something. Do you want to go out now and take photos?"

"Yes. We're going to bring this up with Chad tomorrow, see if we can open an investigation that links the two cases. This one is on our database because the woman who went missing is a witch, but at this stage, it's not serious enough for us to take it off the regular police. It could be a case of a human committing the crimes, and we don't have the resources to chase up something as low level as one woman going missing."

My mouth dropped open. "Something as low level? Are you kidding? How is a woman going missing low level?"

"Sorry. That's not what I meant. I was talking from the point of view of our organisation. If we thought it was a serial killer, or both victim and criminal were witches, we'd be straight on it, but more and more, they're letting the regular police deal with it until they hit a dead end. It's not right, but there's nothing I can do about it right now." He nudged my arm gently with his elbow. "I came here to get you, didn't I? I want to make this a case we're following up on."

Gah, how could I not love this guy? He always did the right thing, and I was silly for thinking he didn't care enough. "Sorry. You're right. Thanks for knowing it's important."

He shook his head. "Don't thank me, Lily. It's my job, and I'm human—I care about everyone. Why else would I do this job?" His jaw tensed. "Unfortunately, not everyone at the PIB shares my enthusiasm. Chad and one director in particular are making things as hard as possible, but we're not going down without a fight."

That escalated quickly. From what Will said, the good agents at the PIB were under attack from the inside. And while we knew things had been worsening for Angelica, we thought everyone else was sort of safe for now. Worry burrowed in my gut. "Going down? What do you mean? Are they shutting the PIB down? They can't!"

He stroked Abby's back, maybe trying to calm himself. "Not yet, they're not, but I wouldn't put it past them. Maybe funding is harder to get? I have no idea, but what I do know is that we've never had this many budget cuts and interference by pencil pushers. It's not the agency I signed up with when I was twenty. That's for sure." He sighed. "Let's drop this, please. It's not constructive, and I need you to get ready so we can go take some photos and hopefully crack a case."

What would happen if the PIB folded? Who would chase witch criminals? There was no way they could get rid of the PIB, was there? Gah, why was everything so damned complicated? I took a deep breath, shook off the despair, and saluted. "Yes, boss." I smiled. "No more negativity, I promise. It's just that I worry about everyone, including Angelica."

He assumed his best poker face. "I'm afraid there's no discussing that."

Huh? "Didn't you talk to James?"

"No, and I'm not going to. Remember a little while ago, she asked us to not worry?"

It took some thinking, but it finally came to me. It had been a subtle conversation. "And you think it's related to wherever she is now?"

"It could be."

"Aren't you even a little bit worried?" His face didn't move an atom. I was betting he was as worried as I was, but he'd never admit it, especially if she'd made him promise not to chase her up. Looked like I wasn't getting anything out of him. Fine. It wouldn't be easy, but I'd hide my concern under a pile of activity. It was time to distract myself because I couldn't do anything to help Angelica right this minute. I stood and magicked my uniform and black coat on. My camera popped into my hand. "Ready."

He gently placed Abby on the couch and stood. She curled

into a ball and shut her eyes. At least someone was relaxed. "We'll go back to headquarters and drive from there."

We made our doorways and stepped through to the PIB reception room. Will buzzed, and the new guy answered. "Agent Blakesley." He gave him a nod. Will nodded back, then walked into the hallway. Then Tommy's eyes caught mine, and he grinned one of those goofy, happy-to-see-you smiles that had danger written all over it. "Lily! Great to see you again."

My return smile was tentative as Will stared at Tommy and wrinkled his forehead. I made sure my tone wasn't nearly as enthusiastic as his had been, but I made sure to keep it amiable. It's not like it was my fault he was being so friendly. It wasn't a reason for me to be rude, and truth be told, I was flattered. Who wouldn't be with a gorgeous guy looking legit happy to see them? "Hey, Tommy. How's your day been?" Will turned a glare on me. I pretended not to notice. It was a question I would've asked Gus, had he been the one answering the door.

Will stepped closer. "Good to see you have your badge on this time."

Tommy touched the badge that sat over his right pec. "Yep. Finally remembered it. There's so much to take in. Feel free to let me know if I get things wrong—I want to learn." Well, that wasn't the response I'd been expecting. Thank goodness this guy wasn't easily offended.

Will's expression relaxed. Not that it went all sprawling on the couch, top-jeans-button-undone-after-a-big-meal relaxed, but at least his poker face was on, which meant calmness would prevail no matter how annoyed he was. "Will do." He looked at me. "Coming? We have work to do." His irritated tone was almost enough to get a reaction, but I didn't think sarcastically saluting him and undermining his authority in front of the new guy was a clever tactic, so I swallowed my irritation… for now.

"Let's go." I made a point of smiling at Tommy. "Have a great afternoon." His return smile was nothing short of radiant. I hoped it burned Will's retinas, and by the way his footsteps echoed loudly down the corridor, my arrow had pierced its mark. Thankfully we didn't have to wait in cranky silence too long as the lift was already on our floor. As soon as we got in and the door closed, I turned to Will. "Look, buddy, it's not my fault the guy was nice to me. And it's not like you to get jealous. You know you can trust me." I shook my head. "Honestly, would you have preferred I was rude to him?"

He folded his arms. "Maybe. I just didn't like how he looked at you. I don't trust him."

I cocked my head to the side. He was being so protective. "This isn't like you. Is everything okay?"

"I'm fine. It's not me we have to worry about."

I rolled my eyes. The lift stopped at B2, and we got out. "Why are you being so weird about this? You know I love you. I'm not looking at anyone else like that."

He blew out a forceful breath. "I know. I'm sorry. It's just, he's so obviously into you, and I don't like it. He didn't even try to hide the fact that he likes you. Did you see how big his stupid grin was?"

I chuckled. Poor Will. I knew how he felt though. It wasn't as if women didn't throw themselves at him sometimes, but I trusted him. "It's not like he knows we're together. We don't pash on at work."

He stopped walking and looked down at me. "Pash on?"

"You know… kiss, like full-on kiss." My cheeks heated. *Seriously, Lily*. It's not like we were talking about sex. This was just kissing. When had I become such a prude?

He smirked. "Oh, you mean like this." He grabbed me around the waist and pulled me to him… and pashed the hell out of me. We were both out of breath by the time he pulled back.

I cleared my throat and fanned my face. "Ah, yeah, like that."

He grabbed my hand and led me to the Range Rover. Seemed like we were all good now. It didn't take much, apparently. I grinned as he opened the door for me. "I'll keep you." He raised a brow at my comment, and I chuckled. He shook his head before shutting my door and going around to the driver side.

Once he got in and started the car, he looked at me. "We're off to Maidstone. Her friends said goodbye to her at The Source Bar. We'll start there, just in case whoever it was followed her. Her friends said she was by herself when she left, and they didn't see anyone go after her—not that that means much. They were all a bit sozzled at the time."

"As you should be when out at a bar having fun." We drove out of the car park and to the security checkpoint, then out onto the street. "I suppose drinking is all fun and games until someone gets attacked. She shouldn't have left by herself. What a crappy world we live in where we have to consider things like that. Why can't everyone just be nice?"

Will frowned. "I wish I knew, Lily. I wish I knew. At least

we're trying to even things up. The more evil people we put away, the better."

"That's for sure." I crossed my fingers that we wouldn't take long to find this evil person. "What's her name?"

"Who?"

"The woman who went missing from The Source."

"Jasmine Harris."

"Thanks." I wanted to know her name because it made her more than a missing person or a statistic. Her name was Jasmine, and she was a real person with thoughts, feelings, friends, and family. "Did she have any pets?"

He flicked a quick gaze towards me before concentrating on the road. "I have no idea. Why?"

Sadness filled my chest, its heaviness drawing me further down into my seat. "If she did, they'd miss her. It's not like the average person can explain to an animal that their person is gone."

"Well, at least she's a witch, so if she did have any pets, hopefully someone has explained it to them."

"Oh, yeah, right. I forgot." I sat up straighter again. "Then how come it's so easy for them to go missing? I mean, witches have power. Surely we can at least assume it's another witch. There's no way a non-witch could take a witch down, unless they shot them from behind without warning, and there were no obvious gunshot wounds in that picture I took."

"There might have been. It's not like that picture was clear. Also, it's not unheard of for people to spike drinks. A witch would be just as helpless if they'd been drugged."

"But in order to have been drugged, it would've had to have happened before she left the club… Jasmine, I mean. Her friends didn't mention she was dragged out by someone, so I'm assuming she was at least capable of using her magic when she was confronted."

"Yes and no. Witches are like normal people—well, they are people, just with added benefits. We all have the fight or flight response. For some people, that means being equipped to deal with a threat, so running or fighting back viciously, but for others, it means freezing. A witch can still lose their ability to think straight in a stressful situation." He put his blinker on to turn right.

I mulled over that the rest of the way to Maidstone, and I made sure my return to sender was up. Now wasn't the time to forget any precautions.

A shiver vibrated down my spine as I stared out into the grey day. There was something about this case, something we hadn't discovered yet, that had me on edge more than usual. Was it because the women were young, like me? It could've been me walking home from a night out with friends, or even getting into an Uber and getting a lift home with a kidnapper or killer.

Finally, Will put his blinker on again and pulled into a car space in front of Maidstone NatWest Bank. A steady stream of shoppers strolled along the footpath. Across the road was a rather swish looking monument of a woman in long robes standing in what looked like the ornate bit of something the pharaohs would've been carried in. Yes, my descriptive powers needed work. The box thingie was churchie-looking and came to a long point on the top after a few ornate flourishes along the way. A slim cross sat atop the whole thing. "Who's that?" I asked.

Will followed my gaze. "Queen Victoria."

"Ah, cool."

Will's eyes flicked to the rear-view mirror, then around the street, to the left and right. He patted his hip. Was he checking for his gun?

Another shiver raced down my arms. "Are you expecting danger? It's the middle of the afternoon."

"Just a feeling." His eyes met mine. "Nothing I can pinpoint, but be alert. Okay?"

"Okay." I opened my door and slid out of the car, ready to grab my magic if needed. As much as I hated the auras, I made sure I watched with my second sight. If there was an ambush from witchy quarters, I'd need to know what spells they had activated. Of all the people walking past, only a couple were witches. Unfortunately, that fact didn't comfort me as much as it should've.

Will came around to stand with me on the footpath. He nodded at a laneway. "The Source is down there."

"What an apt name. Is it a club just for you-know-whats?"

He smiled. "Predominately, but sometimes, they let normal people in too. They have one night a week for mixed nights, but if you notice when we're near, they have a don't-care spell on the façade."

As we walked down Rose Yard—weird name for a paved laneway with no plants, but whatever—we had to sidestep people coming the other way. "What the hell is a don't-care spell? Can you use it for a bad-hair day? Bad hair, don't care?" I snorted at my excellent joke.

Will side-eyed me briefly, then flicked his gaze back to the path ahead. "It causes non-you-know-whats to have absolutely no desire to even know what's in the building, let alone visit it. It means we can stay safe in plain sight. The less we mingle, especially in relationships, the safer we'll all be." It was news I'd heard before, but segregation? That was something I hadn't expected.

"Okay. That sounds reasonable. Is that it?" I stood at the edge of the path, trying to be out of the way of the trickle of people passing through as I checked out the three-storey building. The first two floors were dark-painted rendered brick, and the top floor was an orangey, old brick. Even nightclubs were full of character here. A covered balcony off the first floor hung over the main entry and provided a relaxed-looking drinking spot for patrons, although at this time of year, you'd need an outdoor heater to tempt me.

"Yep, but did you have to stop right here?" Will wrinkled his nose.

"Ew, sorry. My bad. I was too busy looking at the building." I'd managed to stand next to a few industrial-size bins. My nose was obviously asleep on the job. As soon as I realised where we were, the odour hit me full force, and I gagged. Will nudged my back, and we hurried to a spot away from the refuse.

"We're refusing the refuse!" I grinned.

Despite his best efforts, his mouth curled into a smile. "Your jokes are so, so bad. Rubbish, actually."

I giggled. "Nice one! Where have your puns *bin* all this time?"

He groaned and held his hands up. "I can't beat that. I'm done. My pun game is trash." He winked and pew pewed me with both hands.

"Offal with you!" *Beat that, buddy*. I smirked and pointed back the way we'd come. Then I froze, my heart stuttering before beating a million times a minute.

"Lily, what's wrong?"

I opened my mouth, but nothing came out. It was like a nightmare where you couldn't speak or move. Magic prickled my scalp, but it wasn't Will's. It was *hers*.

Dana's smile was all teeth, just like the piranha she was. "Cat got your tongue? Or should I say snake?" She had a no-notice spell as well as a return to sender—no wonder the people in this narrow space weren't paying us the slightest attention.

Will jumped to stand in front of me, blocking my view of Piranha. His magic tingled my scalp, and a near-transparent, shimmering ice-blue shield formed around us.

She laughed. "Ooh, scared of me, are you? Worried your girlfriend's return to sender won't be strong enough against my superior power?"

I peered around Will to see my enemy. The witch looked just as gorgeous as always—shiny, straight black hair to her shoulders, slim figure with ample boobs, which was all shown off by tight leather trousers and a figure-hugging black jumper. I sniffed the air. "Oh, silly me. I thought that horrid odour was coming from the bins." I smiled and raised my chin enough that I could look along my nose at her. "You're such a cliché."

Anger glinted in her eyes, slicing through her amusement. "Keep your pet in line, my darling, or she could get hurt… or worse."

The fact that she wasn't going to ask for clarification on my comment irked. "You wish he was your darling. That ship sailed a long time ago. Oh, and do you want to know why you're a cliché so you can avoid it in future?"

"Lily," Will hissed. "Can you not provoke her?"

"Nope. No can do." I looked at our irritated tagalong. "Okay, since you're not going to ask, I'll tell you, generous person that I am. You're wearing all black. Why do evil people think they look more intimidating in that non-colour of colours? It's not like every teenager didn't go through an angsty black phase—I went through one myself." I held up my coat-clad arm. "Oh, look; I'm in black too! Maybe we all have an evil streak." I smiled, hopefully hiding the fact that my racing heart was pumping in anticipation of my feet getting me the hell out of there ASAP. It was a monumental effort to stay where she could see me and not hide behind Will again.

She narrowed her eyes and folded her arms. "Why aren't you screaming on the ground?" Huh? Oh, crap. My tattoo. They weren't supposed to know we'd deactivated most of it.

"My shield stops you manipulating her tattoo. Your brilliant magic isn't without its flaws." Phew, saved by Will's quick thinking. I touched his back in thanks.

She tilted her head to the side. "Oh, but you can't hold a shield like that forever. You're leaking so much power, my love."

Will tensed. "To be honest, I have far better things to do with my day than waste time talking to a criminal. You're under arrest for mass poisoning and attempted murder." Handcuffs appeared in his hand, and he took a step forward.

She sneered—such a villainy thing to do. So predictable. "Not long now, Will darling, and your pathetic charity case will be no more. I feel it's only fair that she pays for what she took from me." She stared at me, hatred darkening her brown eyes to black. "Soon, you'll end up just like your mother." She cackled—so witchy. "Your witch of a mother killed my mother, and you murdered the man I love. But vengeance will be mine, and it's coming. Enjoy your last weeks on earth, convict witch." What the hell had she said about my mother? I blinked, trying to process it.

Piranha drew her magic, its darkness crawling down my scalp to my spine. Looked like processing would have to wait. I stepped forward, taking in more of my own magic, but Will grabbed my hand. He shook his head and held up the cuffs. Was he suggesting I should wait here while he arrested her?

"But she's drawing so much power, Will. She could be about to do anything." My heart galloped, and my fingers itched to strike her down with lightning, but her return to sender meant I'd be an idiot for trying. But she was right there. So close, yet so far.

"We have our return to senders up and my shield. She's goading you into coming out. Just stand firm." Sweat cast a sheen on his forehead—he was expending so much energy holding the shield up. Would it take much for Piranha to destroy it?

Anger vibrated inside me. How dare she come here and accuse my mother of killing hers? And why should we cower from her? We were just here doing a job. I was so sick of being scared, of having to take precautions. What the hell had I ever done to anyone? Okay, so I'd killed a few people, but they'd mostly deserved it.

She stuck her middle finger up, then raised her other hand to the sky. A doorway formed behind her. As she stepped through backwards, she swung her arm down, calling a streak of silver from the heavens.

Piranha disappeared through her doorway as the lightning struck our shield.

Ear-splitting thunder cracked. Yellow and blue sparks shot across the laneway. People screamed. I slammed into the ground on my side amidst a blinding flash, pain spearing from my shoulder into my neck. Dust and debris peppered my body, and the stench of garbage permeated the air. Will groaned next to me, but he was already sitting up. "Are you all right?"

"My shoulder hurts, but I think I'm okay." I looked along my body, then at my hands. No red stuff, and no pain below my shoulder. My camera had survived the impact, too, thank the universe. But we were surrounded by food scraps, leaves of paper, glass fragments, and stones. Ash fluttered down to land on everything. The impact had shaken the whole laneway. And was that a dead rat? I looked away from the poor critter.

Will's shield was gone, destroyed in Piranha's explosion of power. Maybe putting up a shield had been a mistake? Because of that, she didn't have to worry about our return to senders.

Will swore and said a few choice things about his ex. Once he'd calmed somewhat, he said, "Sit up slowly but don't try and stand just yet. I'm going to call headquarters and check out her departure spot." Will stood and pulled out his phone. He made his call as he walked to where that evil witch had disappeared.

I took his advice and sat up ever so carefully. Once I'd established I wasn't dizzy, I looked around. A handful of dazed pedestrians were taking stock of their surroundings and bodies, shock on their faces. One man limped, and a woman stumbled to her feet using a brick building for support. Blood dripped down the side of her face from a gash. Another woman put her hand to her forehead, as if she was nursing a headache. Windows had blown out on The Source, a mess of glass sprinkled across the laneway. At the opening to the street, a crowd had gathered to stare, a few of them hurrying towards me and the other walking wounded.

I checked myself. My no-notice spell had dropped in the blast. Or maybe her magic had destroyed it? Damn. At least my return to sender was still up.

A young man stopped in front of me and crouched. "Are you okay?"

I nodded carefully, after which relief warmed my insides— still no headache. Phew. "Yes, thanks. Just a sore shoulder, but I'm okay."

His forehead wrinkled. "What happened?" He raised his head to look past me, likely looking for the source of the blast.

I shook my head. "I have no idea. I was just walking along; then there was a flash. Maybe a gas tank blew?" Things were going to be hard to keep a lid on. Would the PIB try to shut this down with mind wipes, or would they let the public come up with their own theories to this mystery? No doubt all the security cameras in the laneway had been rendered useless after Piranha's violent display. If not, I would imagine Will was taking care of that right now. He'd put his phone back in his pocket and was striding down to the other end of the street. Looked like he'd recovered from any soreness after being thrown to the ground, or maybe it was his agent training kicking in—he was definitely physically capable.

"Would you like some help?" The kind stranger stood and held out his hand.

"Thanks." I let him help me up because it was polite. "Maybe you should check on some of the others." When he turned to investigate the situation, I reinstated my no-notice spell. He spun back to me. His eyes briefly rested on me, but then he shook his head and walked off. I was sure he could still see me, but he didn't think to say goodbye. Weird how these spells worked.

Will stood further down the lane, talking to two middle-aged men. His magic tingled my scalp. A minute later, the men nodded and walked towards me, past, then out into the main street. Will gave me a strained smile, then approached the woman who'd been rubbing her head. He must've been doing damage control. I didn't think mind wiping was his specialty, but I guessed he had to act fast, and no one else was here. Ma'am would've been a great help about now. I sighed. Where was she? Was she okay? Gah, I hated not knowing.

While Will dealt with everyone who'd been around when things had gone pear-shaped, I figured I should take the photos that'd brought us here in the first place. I stayed where I was—I could get a wider view of The Source and the laneway—and took the lens cap off my Nikon. A sharp stab seared my shoulder. Crap. Bloody Piranha. I gritted my teeth, turned my camera on, and lifted it to my face. I needed to do this before other PIB agents appeared. "Show me the last time Jasmine Harris left here."

The velvety hand of darkness descended. I panned my camera up to the sky. Stars shone out of the clear night. Focussing back into the lane, the moonlight and illumination from the club gave me a semi-clear view of the smattering of club-goers smoking and chatting in the ally. A couple of the young women had midriff tops and short skirts on. It was ridiculously freezing. What were they thinking? I shivered even though I wore long pants and a coat—and it wasn't even night-time in the real world. Crazy young people. Hmm, I was a crazy young person, but not so crazy that I didn't know how to dress at night-time in the middle of cold weather. Maybe I was the weird one. Who knew? In this, I was happy to be different. They could keep their icy abs.

After scouring the vicinity for our girl, I found her. She'd just exited the club and was about four feet from the door. She wore jeans and a black halter-neck top. Forever captured in a moment in time, she had one arm straight and out to the side as she slid it into the sleeve of her denim jacket. I snapped off a shot and took a few different angles, making sure I got everyone in the laneway into a shot as well. I turned and faced the opening to the street and took more photos. Was our guy watching from the shadows?

Someone tapped me on the back, and I jumped. My shoulder throbbed as I turned to see who it was. Will. A grey splotch of dusty dirt smeared his black trouser leg. "I've taken care of all the cameras. Only one of three was taken out in the power surge." Is that what he was calling it? Seemed more like an explosion.

"Does that mean you've wiped all the evidence too?"

"Yep. Did you get anything?"

"Yep." I handed him the camera. Another bolt of pain in my shoulder made me flinch.

His brow furrowed. "What's wrong?"

"Just the shoulder. As soon as we get back, I'll see Beren."

"Good. We won't be long here. I just want to brief the team. There's an undercover pair nearby. Should be here any moment."

On cue, two male agents strode into the laneway. They were dressed in plain clothes, but their witch auras and muscular statures, together with their self-assured countenances, told me everything I needed to know. Will approached them, and they had a little chat before Will returned to me. "Okay. Let's go."

Even though Will had done a relatively good job of making sure this wasn't going to turn into an incident, two of the injured bystanders were standing around, looking confused. I nodded towards them. "Are they going to be okay?"

"The new agents will see to them." Sirens sounded in the distance. "Let's get out of here. I don't want to have to explain. Our guys will take care of everything. It's their specialty." He grabbed my hand, and we hurried out of the laneway and to his car. He stopped without warning and pulled my hand, halting my forward trajectory and jerking me backwards.

"Ow! What the hell?" As if the pain in my shoulder wasn't bad enough, he had to try and rip my arm from its socket. Sheesh.

"Look at my car… carefully, and tell me what you see."

My other sight was still activated. I used it and stared. Interestingly, or maybe not because they weren't living things, cars had no auras. I was about to say I couldn't see anything when the air around the car shimmered briefly, like it did above the road on a hot day. After a few seconds, the shimmer did its thing again. We stood there for a minute, watching the pulse beat a steady rhythm. I turned and spied other cars parked nearby, and they had no shimmer. Right, so it wasn't something all cars did that I'd missed because, well, I wasn't the most observant person. "What is it?"

"A bomb."

My heart dropped into my stomach, and I swallowed. My voice was hoarse. "A bomb?"

"Yes. A magical one, of course, but the end result is the same." His grip on my hand tightened for a moment, then relaxed. The muscle in his jaw ticked as he stared at his beloved Range Rover.

"Now what?" I assumed he'd do something because standing here all night wasn't going to achieve much. "Does it go off if someone touches the car?" If that was the case, everyone walking around here was in danger. Crap.

"No. If she wanted to make sure of killing us, she'd set it to go off once we'd gotten in and shut both doors. It's a complicated spell that would've taken at least an hour to construct."

"But how could she have done that? We weren't parked there for an hour."

"It's possible to construct a spell and deploy it later, but it's complicated and takes a lot of power, plus, if you lose concentration and the spell unravels before you place it, you could blow yourself up."

"Right. So she went to a lot of trouble. But how could she know when we were going to go somewhere? If what you say is true, she couldn't have made it last week in anticipation of us going somewhere."

"She would have watched and known I'd driven to work

today. She could make the spell every time, for all I know, and wait to see if you're in the car with me when I leave. It's dangerous, but she's crazy and single-minded enough to do that."

Wow, she hated me just about as much as it was possible to. "So she sat there for a good portion of the day just waiting for this opp?"

"Yep." He looked down at me, anger and worry blazing from his grey eyes. "This is worse than I thought, Lily. I thought, at first, that her father wanted you for your power, but this changes everything. She wants you dead, no matter what her father wants."

"Do you think she's the rogue element that message spoke of?"

"Yes. It all makes sense. She's behind those RP thugs coming to get you—I'd bet my life on it. What her father wants is another mystery."

I licked my bottom lip, trying to think things through. "Why do you think she said my mother killed hers? I mean, we saw in those photos I took that night with Beren, that her father killed her mother."

"They weren't conclusive. We saw her father burn their house down with their mother inside. But she was already unconscious, or maybe even dead when he did that. You didn't photograph a killing blow, did you?"

"No." Crap. Nausea swished in my stomach and seized my throat. I forced it back down with a hard swallow, then took a deep breath. "I can't believe my mother would kill someone, and why?"

Will raised a brow, an incredulous expression on his face.

"You've killed many people. How is this any different? She was an agent for many years, Lily. She was trained to kill."

I took another deep breath. Of all the times for Will to be right, now was not the time I wanted. But he spoke the truth. My mother was a trained killer, just like Will, Beren, Angelica, Imani—my friends. I shook my head. But it was for the good of humanity. They weren't cold-hearted murderers, and neither was I. "Maybe her father killed her mother and blamed my mother because he didn't want to upset his daughter?"

He considered that for a moment. "Possibly. But there's no way to prove anything right now. I need to deal with this."

"How long will it take to unravel the spell?"

"An hour, a day? I don't know."

"Can you tow it?"

"Possibly, but I doubt it." He handed my camera back, swore, then pulled his phone out and made a call. After that, we waited for his colleagues and the regular police to turn up and cordon off the street. A witch bomb specialist started on the spell while I stood and watched Will pace up and down the footpath until his phone rang. "Agent Blakesley speaking." He harrumphed, swore again, and hung up. He turned to me. "Come on, I'm taking you to headquarters."

"So Beren can heal my shoulder?"

"Yes… and I've been called in for a talking-to by Chad. This is going to be fun." His eyes were the colour of the angriest storm cloud. His brows drew down, and a five-o'clock shadow framed his pinched lips. As he led me to the nearest public toilet, I'd never hated Piranha more. And when our two hatreds collided, whatever explosion she'd had planned for Will and me in his car was going to seem like a puff of dust.

She'd crossed my line a long time ago, and now she'd gone so far over it, she was in dangerous territory. When the time came for our showdown, I wasn't going to hold back. She brought out the person in me I feared the most. And that person was going to kill her if she got half a chance.

Who was I, and what had I done with the naïve and innocent Lily who'd arrived in the UK a year ago?

The sad part was, as much as I didn't want to find out, it was inevitable, and the time was near. In order to have a new beginning in life, the old life had to die. Unfortunately, new didn't mean better. I shivered as I stepped into a toilet cubicle and made my doorway.

There was no turning back. And the most chilling thing? Whatever transpired, I was committed to this. I wanted it to happen.

Who was I, indeed?

CHAPTER 5

On arrival at the PIB, Tommy greeted us. His extra happy smile for me elicited a grunt from Will, but he said nothing as we hurried to Beren's office so my shoulder could be fixed. Will left me with Beren while he attended the meeting with Chad. As soon as Will shut the door, Beren worked on my injury. It took about ten minutes for him to fix it.

He looked at me. "How does it feel?"

I shrugged, moved my arm around, and then poked at the injury with my hand. I smiled. "Perfect. Thank you, Dr Beren."

"Good." His smile quickly dissipated. "What's going on with Will? He didn't look too impressed when he left here."

I made a bubble of silence. "He got called in to see the ultimate agent of stupid. I'm not sure why. It might have some-thing to do with what happened this afternoon." Chad had likely got wind of things as soon as Will had called in the attack. News travelled faster than a dad joke at a family get-together around here.

"I heard something happened, but I haven't had time to stop and listen. So spill."

"Dana happened."

His mouth dropped open. "What?"

"Yes, exactly. Will and I were out investigating something, and she turned up, caused a scene, tried to kill us with lightning, then left. Oh, and just to make sure, she also put a bomb spell on Will's car."

Beren's brows drew down; then he shook his head. "Surely she didn't think he'd miss that. Maybe it was just a warning?"

"Or maybe she's crazy and desperate to kill me. She thinks my mother killed hers. She took great pains to tell me that today." Anger heated my stomach and vibrated in my chest. "I mean, we saw that it wasn't my mother, right?"

He cocked his head to the side. "Yes and no. She wasn't there when the house went up, but we don't know what happened before that."

"But I asked my magic. It would've shown her, surely?" My magic hadn't done wrong by me yet. I had to trust it. Besides, if I had to choose between believing Piranha or my magic, it was a no-brainer.

"True." He leaned back in his chair and folded his arms. "I'm just wondering why now? Why is she showing herself at this particular time?"

"I have no idea. Maybe she's having a bad day and her grief got the better of her? I killed the love of her life, apparently." I sighed. "Maybe that was unfair of me, but honestly, he tried to kill me for goodness' sake. What was I supposed to do? If she doesn't want the love of her life to die, don't send him to kill me. End of story."

Beren smiled. "Save your sympathy for those who deserve it." He unfolded his arms and leaned forward, intensity shining from his eyes. "And don't you ever, ever soften your heart against Dana. You give her the smallest opening, and she'll use it. You can't afford any remorse, any sympathy where she's concerned. And if you're compromised, Will, I, Imani, any of us will jump in to save you. One of us could die need-lessly if you let your guard down." He took a breath and sat back. "Stay tough, Lily. Our lives all depend on it."

My voice was smaller than I'd intended when I said, "Okay." But what was there to say? I knew I would kill her given half the chance. Until she was dead, I'd be in danger, and so would my brother and niece. She'd threatened my whole family. The searing anger from before returned, burning into my memory. I would. Not. Forget. I sat up straight and made my voice strong. "I won't let my guard down, B. You have my word."

He gave a firm nod. "So, changing the subject… what were you guys investigating?"

"Two women have gone missing recently. One was someone I saw through my phone in the background on TV. After I saw her, Will did some digging and came up with another woman who went missing in similar circumstances. We were checking it out, seeing if we could get enough evidence to link them so Will could get approval to launch a proper investigation."

"Did you find anything?"

I shrugged, happy that my shoulder didn't so much as twinge. "I don't know. I took a few snaps of her as she was leaving a nightclub, and I took pics of everyone in the laneway at that time, but Piranha came and messed everything up. We had to abandon it when the other agents arrived. It was a disaster. We still have to check out her walk home. I have no idea when that's going to happen." I bit my fingernail. "You don't think the ultimate agent of stupid is going to fire Will, do you?"

He scrunched his face in a "you've got to be kidding" way. "For what? No doubt, he'll have a whinge over wasting resources and send him on his way."

I looked at the time on my phone. "He's been gone for twenty minutes. That's a long time for such an uncomplicated chat." Worry slithered in my gut.

"Maybe he wanted to chat about the weather?" He ruined his false bravado by looking at the door expectantly. Funnily enough, it opened, and Will strode through, his face stony.

"Since when are you psychic, B?"

"Since now." He stood from his spot next to me and gestured at Will to sit in the guest's chair, then went around and sat on the other side of his desk. Will, jaw muscles bunched, sat with a thud.

I gingerly reached out to lay a hand on his arm. "What the hell happened? Are you okay?"

A knock sounded on the door. "Come in," said Beren.

Tommy entered, and Will's scowl deepened. Wow, could this day get any better? Tommy gave a nod to Beren. "Sorry to interrupt. I've been sent to collect Lily. Agent Williamson the

Third wants to talk to her." He looked down at me and smiled. I glanced nervously at Will.

"I have no idea, Lily, but I imagine it won't be good." I took his intense stare as a warning to watch myself in there. Would've been good to know what happened between Chad and Will, but Chad acted fast, sending Tommy to get me without warning. Will stood and looked at Tommy. "I'm coming with you."

Was that annoyance that flicked across Tommy's face? "Your call, Agent Blakesley. I doubt you'll be allowed in the meeting, but you can walk with us."

Will looked down at me. "Come on."

I took his proffered hand, blew out a breath, and stood. I looked at Tommy. "Take me to your leader." Okay, so I couldn't help making light of a stressful situation, but I only managed a wan smile. I just wasn't feeling it. Why did Chad want to talk to me? It so couldn't be good. I had to remember that I wasn't an agent. He had no power over me. But what if he put a spell on me to make me talk? It was illegal, but still… it wasn't like people never broke the law. If they followed legalities all the time, the PIB would be out of business.

"Good luck." Beren gave me a "what are you gonna do?" look.

"Thanks. We'll come back here as soon as I'm done." My voice was a lot lighter than I felt. Cement blocks of fear encased my feet. I stared at the chair I'd just vacated, wanting to drop into it again and stay there.

"Come on." Tommy led the way to the door—which was still open from when he came in. Will pulled me along and out into the hallway. He squeezed my hand reassuringly, but neither of us spoke. Giving away our secrets to Tommy was not an option. I'd just have to suffer the unknown for a couple of minutes. At least this—whatever it was—would be over soon.

Instead of taking us to the normal conference room, Tommy took us to the third floor, which was the top of the tree at the PIB. I frowned. My stress meant I couldn't even enjoy my stupid rhyme. What had my life become? Okay, I was being melodramatic, but it'd been a ridiculously challenging day.

We exited the lift, then continued along another corridor. My desperate and slightly laboured breaths punctuated the beat of our marching footsteps. Even though Will was holding my hand, I felt like I was being dragged to the gallows. Why was I so scared? It was normal to laugh off Chad's idiocy, but coming so close on the heels of Will's meeting…. Did he just want to ask me about the incident with Piranha? Maybe that's all it was, but if so, why had Will looked so angry when he'd returned? Surely he didn't know about my photographic talent. My eyes widened. What if he didn't but he was going to magic all my secrets out of me?

Will squeezed my hand again, bringing me out of my panic loop. I squeezed it back and gave him a hopeless smile.

Tommy stopped at the end of the corridor. We'd reached the end of the line. But there was nothing here. Just three white walls and a flickering fluorescent light. So annoying. Tommy and Will stared at each other. After several moments, Tommy said, "You can wait here." What, we were going to leave him here and walk back the way we'd come? That was kind of like putting him in the naughty corner.

Will grunted, then tore his gaze from Tommy and looked at me. "Good luck. You got this. If something happens and you're scared, call out for me. I'll be here."

"What if he puts up an absolute bubble of silence?"

"Don't worry. I'll know. I have a sixth sense where you're concerned." He winked and gave me a small smile.

I couldn't help but smile in return. He made things so much better, and if I wasn't mistaken, he was hinting that I should contact him mind to mind. We hadn't used it since we'd discovered we could talk to each other that way because we didn't want RP finding out. We needed all the secret ammunition we could get when it came to them. Who knew what awaited us when we finally cracked that case wide open?

"Enough of the chit-chat." Tommy's voice was all business, but when he looked at me, his gaze softened. "Don't worry, Lily. You'll be fine. Agent Blakesley isn't the only one who's looking out for you."

Okay, and that wasn't super awkward. I mean, what girl wouldn't want two gorgeous men in her corner? But seeing as how I'd made my choice, there wasn't room for someone else, even if he did have the most stunning blue eyes. *Okay, Lily, that's quite enough*. I cleared my throat and risked a glance at Will before meeting Tommy's stare. "Ah, thanks."

Tommy smirked, as if he'd wanted to irritate Will, or as if he'd somehow won a point. "Through here." Tommy's magic caressed my scalp. It was smooth and subtle, but there were other notes just under the surface, ones I couldn't grasp. A door formed in the wall and opened inward, revealing a red-carpeted stairway with a gold-coloured bannister flanked by the requisite white walls. A few small paintings hung there, their gold and timber frames marking them as potentially expensive artwork. So strange. "After you."

I turned and gave Will a small wave, swallowed my trepidation, and went through. Invisible feathers tickled my face and front, like when you walk through those old-fashioned rubber streamers hanging from a doorway. One of Dad's friends owned an Italian grocery shop near the city, at Leichhardt, in Sydney. We visited a few times, and he had the multi-coloured strips hanging in between the shop and the back storage-cum-workers' lunch space. I used to pretend I'd be walking through into a fairyland. Unfortunately, as had been the case there, no fairy garden would be awaiting me here either. And what was waiting would be way worse than the boring sack of potatoes and bags of produce in Uncle Sergio's storeroom.

I figured that sensation was some kind of warning or protection spell—if you were running a witch law-enforcement agency, surely you had enemies or at least people who hated whoever was in the job. I reached the top of the flight of stairs to another blank wall. Tommy reached the landing and placed his hand on my back, pressing gently to move me out of the way. I ignored the butterflies his touch ignited. He wasn't Will, and while he could be the nicest guy in the world and super good-looking, again, he wasn't Will. I stepped to the side.

His magic feathered my scalp, and another door appeared. He knocked on it—a series of three well-spaced knocks followed by five staccato ones, then a double-hand slap, followed by both hands knocking in a frenzy for a few seconds. You had to be joking. I stifled a laugh. Surely there were security cameras hidden here and Chad knew exactly who was standing outside his door.

After a few moments, the door swung open, care of an agent I'd seen around but had never met—a man, an inch taller than me whose black jacket and pants were bursting with muscle. His shaved head gave him a menacing appearance, and there was no laughter in his green eyes.

"Come in," Chad called from across the immense carpeted room. This was more like a study in an old English mansion than a PIB office. Timber panelling came halfway up the walls, and his large mahogany desk sat in front of a wall of bookshelves. Three windows to his left—likely bulletproof—let in light.

The thirty feet to his desk took what felt like forever. Again, totally awkward and nerve-racking as he watched me walk and walk. Why couldn't this stupid room be smaller? My pulse beat at twice its normal rate. I jammed my teeth together, hating that Chad had this effect on me. Stuff it. I knew Will and anyone else associated with me might be at risk of losing their job because of this guy, but I had nothing to lose. Nothing. If I could make him believe I didn't care about my friends, hopefully he'd decide to leave me alone. Ma'am was already in the crapper, which meant everyone else might soon follow, so it was a risk I was willing to take. And what had he done to her? Even though she hadn't said much, I was sure Chad, or at least the directors of this place, had something to do with it.

I finally made it to his desk, Tommy a few steps behind. I went to sit in one of the three guest chairs in front of the desk, but he held up his hand. "Stop! There will be no sitting." He stood and looked at Tommy. "You can go and wait outside. If I need you, I'll call."

"Yes, Sir." Tommy gave me an encouraging look, then turned and left. Didn't matter how many encouraging looks I got, it was still just me in this room. I had to defend myself, which was hard, considering I had no idea why I'd been called here. Maybe I should've just refused and gone home? I was only a contractor, after all. Hmm, maybe I should just turn and leave.

"Lily? Lily, hello?" Chad had come to my side of the table and stood in front of me, waving a hand in my face.

I shook my head to clear it. "Oh, sorry. I was off with the fairies." Seemed like I *had* walked through into fairyland. Although Chad and his agent friend looked more like ogres than fairies. I bit my tongue to stop from laughing.

Chad pursed his lips, looking at me as if I wasn't quite the full quid. He planted his hands on his hips. "You don't seem concerned about being here."

I raised a brow—blasé was my middle name; at least, that's what I wanted him to think. I shrugged. "Should I be?"

"Should you be what?"

Oh dear. "Concerned."

"Oh, yes, of course. And yes, yes, you should."

I smiled. "Okay. Great!" He blinked and frowned. My smile grew, but I managed to stop the laughter that tried to escape.

His brows drew together. "So why aren't you?"

74

My turn to play stupid, although, to be fair, he might not be playing. "So why aren't I what?"

"Concerned, worried. You've been called into the office of the head of the PIB."

I casually turned and surveyed the room, completing a full circle to look at him again. "Hmm, so I have."

Mouth closed tight, he blew a noisy, frustrated breath out of his nose. "So?" When I shrugged again, his arms pinioned straight by his sides, his hands clamping into white-knuckled fists. "This is not how it was supposed to go."

I waved my hand noncommittally. "Whatever." I plastered an earnest expression on my face. "I do understand your frustration, however. I hate it when things don't go the way I planned. It can be most inconvenient, don't you think?"

He nodded. "Yes, it damned well can. Are all you Ossies so irritating?"

"What's an ossy?"

"Don't play stupid with me. You know what an Ossy is."

Okay, I did know what he meant, but after all the stress he was trying to put me through, and whatever he'd done to Will, he deserved a bit of his own medicine. "I really have no idea." Serenity radiated from my face. Let it not be said that I couldn't poker face with the best of them when I wanted. Hmm, although was this a poker face or something more? I mean, I was actually expressing myself, just not the expression I was feeling.

"An Australian."

"Oh! You mean *Auzzie*. It's spelled with the esses, but you pronounce it with a zee sound. Auzzzzzzzzzzie." I produced my most joyous smile. Funnily enough, none of that joy seemed to have made it to Chad. "Aaaaaanyway. If that's all, can I go now?"

His eyes widened, and he slammed his palm on the desk. "No!" He dropped his head back and stared at the ceiling for a moment, his chest rising and falling with aggressive breaths. He lowered his head and stared at me, anger vibrating from his gaze. "Ask me why I called you here."

"But why?" Pressing people's buttons was such fun. I needed to do it more often. This particular tactic was something that had driven my parents mad. Sadness surprised me with a slap to the face, but I hid it as best I could. There was no way I wanted him to think he'd upset me. The reminder that this was nothing compared to losing my parents gave me even more confidence.

"Because I ordered it!"

"But why?"

His eyes bugged to such an extent that I readied to catch his eyeballs when they shot from his head. "What are you doing?"

"Preparing to catch your eyeballs." Oh my God, did I really just say that? A choked cough came from the other side of the room. We both turned and looked at Tough Agent standing next to the door. He was quick to resume his poker face but not quick enough that I didn't see the smile that preceded it.

Chad felt at both eyes with his fingers. Redness seeped up his neck like a glass being filled with red cordial, until it reached his hairline. I tilted my head to the side. "Um, are you feeling okay? You might want to sit down."

Fists shaking at his sides, he opened his mouth and

screamed. "Arghhhhhhhhhhhh!" When he was done, he looked at me. "Enough! I asked you here because I'm banning you from PIB headquarters. I'm cleaning out of all Angelica's trash. It's a bit difficult to get rid of all of you vermin until I can get replacements, but I can't see what value you add to this organisation. I'm thinking you were here because she wanted to give paid employment to her incompetent friends. You're not to set foot in this place ever again. You will not, ever, accompany any of my agents to any crime scenes. You are hereby excluded from any future contract work." He was breathing hard, as if that tirade had cost him hugely. He leaned close to my face. "So, there."

I pressed my lips together to stop from laughing. It was crappy that he'd banned me, but on the whole, it could've been a lot worse. He didn't know about my talent. My secret was safe... for now. I sucked in a huge breath and let it out... in his face. He narrowed his eyes and leaned back. I smiled. "Phew! I thought it was going to be something terrible. Well, I'm glad that's over with. Anything else?" He glared at me. And glared. And glared. His mouth opened and closed a few times. I cocked my head to the side. "Right, then. Looks like I'll be getting out of your hair. Toodle-pip." I lifted my hand, waggled my fingers in a ditzy wave, and sauntered to the door.

Tough Agent kept his poker face but gave me a nod as he opened the door. Tommy was waiting on the other side. Chad hurried over and pushed in front of me.

I raised my brows, hoping it showed my displeasure. "Ye of little manners." I was already on his bad side. Might as well go the whole way.

He turned and shot me an incensed look. "This is *my* office in an organisation *I* run. I'll do *what* I want to *whom* I want *when* I want." I raised my brows and threw him my best "you've got to be kidding me" look. He narrowed his eyes and turned back to Tommy. "See her out of the building. Make sure she makes her doorway and leaves. She is banned from this building from hereon in. If I see her here again, it will be your job. Understand?"

"Yes, Sir. I won't let you down."

"Good." He spun, making sure not to look at me again, and stomped back to his desk. Tommy and Tough Agent shared a worried look, then pretended nothing had happened.

Tommy sounded apologetic as he spoke. "I'm sorry, but we have to go. You can make your doorway in the hallway downstairs."

"Okay, cool." My nonchalance was all an act, especially now I realised that something had to have happened with Angelica. There was no way Chad would've spoken so openly about getting rid of her favourites if she had any sway at the PIB. I swallowed. What the hell had they done with her, because, let's face it, Chad wasn't behind whatever was going on. And what was going to happen to that case? Surely I could help secretly? Even without the PIB, we could find out what happened and make sure those women got justice, couldn't we? And out of "we," how many were left?

I started down the stairs, Tommy's presence at my back. "Are you okay? Sounds like things got serious in there."

"I guess. I'm not an agent anyway, so I suppose it doesn't matter."

"What about visiting your brother?"

"Yeah, that'll be annoying. In fact, most of the people I care about work here, so that is kind of crappy."

"That's too bad. Maybe you can catch up with them at lunch times. Do you have a favourite café you like to visit? If you're ever up for catching up, I'd love to buy you a coffee. I'm new in town, and I don't know anyone."

I stopped at the bottom and turned to look up at him. He'd stopped on the second-last step. This made things difficult. There was no way I was having coffee with a guy I hardly knew without Will being there. Even though his intentions were likely harmless, it felt like cheating, and I knew I would hate if Will started having coffees with random gorgeous women from work. "Um, I guess, but maybe with Will too. He hates when I don't include him." I chuckled, trying to make it funny rather than awkward. I probably failed.

"Um, oh. Are you two serious, then?"

"Yes. But if you're looking to meet people, Will's a person, and so are our other friends." My smile was genuine this time.

He shrugged. "I suppose that's okay. So, where do you love grabbing coffee?"

"Costa at Westerham. They have the best double-chocolate muffins ever, and the place is always busy and warm. It's kind of like visiting your grandparents and having lots of family and friends around. It's cosy." Hmm, I might be overstating things a bit, but it did have an atmosphere I loved, and it was familiar—one of the most familiar things I had here in the UK. A pang of homesickness hit, and I thought of Surfer's Brew and my favourite barista, Frances. "Next time we go, I'll get Will to let you know… since I can't just drop in here anymore."

"Why don't I get your number?" He pulled out his phone, and I gave it to him. Hopefully Will wouldn't mind. I was just being nice, after all, and what harm could it do?

Hmm, I should've known that if I had to ask that question, something bad was going to come of it. But I was clueless.

Story. Of. My. Life.

CHAPTER 6

I sat on one of Angelica's Chesterfields, Will next to me, and James and Imani sitting on the one opposite. They'd finished work at 7:00 p.m. and had surprised me with an impromptu meeting.

Everything was as bad as I'd feared.

I looked at Will. "I can't believe Chad put you on probation for looking into those cases without his approval. This is crazy." I wanted to scream my anger till I was hoarse, but that would achieve nothing, so I growled—it wasn't as satisfying, but it was better than nothing.

James eyeballed me. "And what exactly happened when he called you in, Lily? Chad took the rest of the afternoon off after speaking to you. Agent Pembury wouldn't say much when I asked, but he did say that you pushed all his buttons and that it was amusing."

Ah, so the serious agent protecting him today was Agent

Pembury. I took it he was on our side since he confided in James. I shrugged. "I was just being me." I grinned.

James chuckled, and Imani snorted. Will, on the other hand, grumbled. "Lily, I'm in enough trouble over there. Please don't make it worse. I know what he did to you is ridiculous and uncalled for, but baiting him isn't going to help the rest of us."

Guilt. What an irritating price to pay. I'd known that their jobs were on the line, but self-control wasn't my strong suit. I grabbed his hand. "I'm sorry, but I'm just as angry as you are, and he also mentioned Ma'am. I was pretty cranky, and I wanted to get my own back. My desire for revenge overcame my common sense. Sorry."

He gave me a lopsided smile. "That's okay. I'm upset, too, and maybe I'm a bit crankier than I should be. At least we know he's easily goadable. And can you back up? What did he say about Ma'am?"

"He said he's cleaning out Angelica's trash." I frowned. Such a simple sentence, but such massive consequences.

Will's jaw muscle ticked, and James's eyes widened. Imani raised a brow and said, "Is that so? That little rat. Not that this is a total surprise, but for him to slip and let that out. He obviously didn't think that through."

"You can thank my poking, poking, poking. I riled him up until he lost it." I chuckled. Such enjoyment even hours later. It was so totally worth it. I'd been waiting all day to know what happened in Will's meeting. "So, you didn't tell me what he said to you."

"You left rather quickly."

"Yeah, well, getting kicked out will make that happen."

He side-eyed me. "Tommy seemed to be in a rush to get you to leave. He didn't even give me a chance to say goodbye."

I shrugged. "I guess he's just doing his job. Chad was adamant that I left ASAP. Besides, it's not like you don't get to come home and see me." I smiled. "So, spill."

"As you've heard, I'm on probation, which means desk duties and research for the foreseeable future. Oh, and some jail duties, like overseeing transport of dangerous prisoners."

My mouth dropped open. "You're kidding. They're relegating you to secretarial and guard duty? Are they hoping you'll quit?"

"Well, considering they're subject to the same unfair dismissal laws non-witches are, probably. But I'm not about to quit. And after that comment about Angelica, I'm going to need access to the database and all the agents at head office. Chad has basically declared war on us. And if he's after me"—he stared at James—"you're next." He looked at Imani. "Then you, Beren, and anyone else who's been one of Ma'am's go-to agents in the last twelve months."

James drummed his fingers on his thigh. "The question is, why? I'm pretty sure it's Brosnan, but what we don't know is whether any of the other directors are involved and what the end game is."

Imani looked thoughtful. "Is it a personal vendetta, or does it go deeper than that? When you look at who they've put in and who they want to get rid of, it reeks of a power play."

That didn't make a lot of sense to me, but then, I wasn't exactly an expert on PIB politics. "But what kind of power play? Surely the directors get paid the same, and their goal would be to stop crime. I mean, why else would you set up the PIB?"

Will looked at me. "Power, Lily. They can help strengthen the PIB to deal with crime, but they can also make sure their buddies—or themselves—are above the law. Maybe they take bribes, maybe they blackmail, and maybe they just like the way people fawn over them when they find out what title they hold. And the biggest kudos of all is to be the most powerful director, the one who really calls the shots and has the final say."

"So, you're saying that it could be internal power plays?" It still didn't ring true for me. Something else could be going on.

Will nodded. "Something like that. Anyway, no matter what it is, we're caught in the middle, and we have to figure out how to fix it."

James and Imani stayed quiet, and even Will didn't look confident. What they were really saying is that whatever was happening was out of our control, and in that case, we had to sit tight and deal with crap when it happened. There was only one problem—okay, there was more than one problem, but the most urgent problem—Ma'am was likely in immediate danger. "Surely Angelica saw this coming." And that was the thing. She wasn't blind or stupid. She must've known what was going on, or at least some of it. *Oh.*

Will smirked at me. "I see by the look on your face that you're finally getting it."

James cocked his head to the side. "Getting what?"

Will looked at James. "We have to keep this quiet, and that's why Angelica didn't say anything to anyone else. She hinted to Lily and me that she might be out of sight for a while. She suggested she was going on holidays, but when has she ever gone on holiday? She also implored us not to worry."

Imani raised a brow. "So she knew. How long ago was this?"

I shrugged. "A few weeks."

Will nodded. "She didn't say anything to anyone else because we have to keep this on a need-to-know basis. I would imagine she's gathering intelligence and figuring out how to stop whatever's going on. They might think they have the better of her, but knowing her, she'll have a nice surprise for them."

Worry emanated from Imani's eyes. "I hope you're right, Will. Angelica's good, but going up against the directors?" She inhaled a deep breath and shook her head.

James shared a concerned look with me. "I want to think on this before I decide how to proceed. We need to tread carefully. As much as I'm concerned, I think we're right to believe she can take care of herself for a bit. We have so much on our plate at the moment, spreading our thinking resources is a mistake, and I imagine that's something else she wanted to avoid. Let's deal with our RP mission first. We can't afford any mistakes there either. Let's all just draw as little attention to ourselves at work as possible." He turned to Imani. "I think we should both avoid headquarters for a couple of days, call in sick."

She nodded. "Okay."

James looked at Will. "You're stuck at headquarters. You can keep your ear to the ground for us."

Will nodded. "Sounds good." He pursed his lips. "While you're 'sick,' maybe Imani could go with Lily and keep on with our investigation into those attacks?"

James frowned. "How is that laying low?"

"They can pretend they're on a shopping day out or something. We already have the photos from outside the venue. Lily won't have to take any photos within a block of there. And if the girls put on some disguises and travel there, no one will be any the wiser, even if Chad has agents watching the site for our return. And by travelling from here, RP won't know where Lily is."

I sat up straight. "Ooh, I could call Lavender, see if he can help us look different." Sarah's make-up-artist friend had become a good friend to all of us. "He's always up for some adventure. Maybe he and Sarah want to come with us, make it look like a more legit shopping expedition. Plus, no one will be looking for four of us."

Imani nodded slowly. "That could work. Good idea, love."

Another idea hit me, but it was scary because it involved one of my best friends. What if I suggested this, and James thought it was a good idea, and then something bad happened? I stared at the table and took a deep breath, mulling.

Will touched my arm gently. "Lily, what's wrong?"

Should I? Damn it. We needed this. I looked up. "I have an idea…."

James raised a brow. "Whenever you say that, things happen. Not necessarily good things."

"Yeah, I know, and this time might not be any different, but I feel I have to say this."

"Okay," Will said. "Spill."

"What if we fake a fight between Liv and Millicent? What if it causes a fallout between Beren and you guys as well? And what if Liv asks to be transferred to someone closer to Chad?"

Imani's brow furrowed. "Asking to go to Chad might be obvious, but maybe to one of his favourites?"

Will looked at me. "That's a great idea, Lily. Dangerous, but good. Maybe I can organise for someone to fall ill for a few days. Why not go straight for Chad's assistant?"

My mouth dropped open. "That's way too dangerous, Will. If you're caught, you'll go to jail."

He fixed on his best poker face. "Yes, true, but we don't have to do this the magic way. A simple case of food poisoning should be enough. I'm sure I can make it happen. And, in fact, maybe James could order the same thing, pretend to be ill, then take his sick leave. That would look even less suspicious."

James smiled. "Genius. Now we have to watch for when and what she eats at the cafeteria."

"Is she a witch?" I asked.

James shook his head. "No. So they probably won't think to heal her. Which is the only flaw in our plan—if they heal her. But even if they decide to use magic on her, she'll be off for at least a day or two—it takes even more out of non-witches as it does witches. They'll definitely want to heal me. I can overplay how tired I am afterwards."

"Oh, that's right." I should've thought of that. "But why wouldn't they heal her?"

Imani frowned. "Because some witches think non-witches are inferior and undeserving. They'll use the excuse that if we do it for one, we have to do it for all, which is total bull.

Although, considering she's Chad's assistant, he may decide she gets special treatment. We'll just have to see. If it doesn't work, we'll come up with something else."

Maybe we needed a Plan B now. "We could try a different way, but it would potentially take too much time."

James tipped his chin up. "Go on, then. What's your idea?"

"We could get Liv to get really chummy with her—since they're both non-witches. Surely they have things to complain about to each other with work and witch bosses. Liv could then offer to help her, tell her she hasn't got much to do for Millicent?"

James smiled. "Great. That's our Plan B, then." He turned to Imani. "I think you should call in sick before then, anyway. I might even contaminate something that goes through the organisation. I mean, contaminating one batch of food won't cause too much trouble, and it'll seem even more legit."

Gee, my brother was more conniving than I'd thought. I only ever saw the caring, big-brother side of him. I supposed you didn't get to his position in a government law enforcement agency being all sunshine and squirrels. Ah, squirrels. I'd have to make time tomorrow to go into the backyard and feed them. I could do with some cheering up.

Will clapped once. "Right. We have our plans. James and I will execute Operation Food Poisoning tomorrow while Imani and Lily get into disguise and gather some evidence. Any questions?" We all shook our heads.

I magicked my phone from my bedroom. "I'd best call your sister now, Will. Make sure they're available for tomorrow. If they're not, we might have to postpone that side of things."

Will looked at me, love in his eyes. "Do whatever you have

to, Lily. I want you safe. We don't have to rush—these cases have been ignored for a while. A day or three won't make much difference."

I smiled. "Thanks." I got on the phone, and Sarah answered within two rings. "Wow, that was fast."

"Hey, Lily! How've you been?"

I grinned. It was so good to hear her voice. "Good, thanks. I was just wondering what you and Lav were up to tomorrow. Are you guys free for a shopping trip?" I wasn't going to spill it all on the phone. We had privacy spells on all our phones, but sometimes, it wasn't enough. Best to be careful.

"I'm free. I'm not sure about Lav, but I'll let him know and get back to you. What time do you want us at yours?"

"Nine is cool. Shops don't open before then anyway. We could grab a coffee, then have at it."

"Lovely. See you tomorrow! I'll text Lav and let you know if there's a problem. Is everything else good?"

"Yep. Everyone's well. I'm sure we'll have a lot to talk about tomorrow. See you then! Night!"

"Say hi to Will for me. Night, lovely."

I hung up and looked at Imani. "Right. We're good to go for tomorrow."

"Excellent, love. I'll be here just before nine."

And that was that. I was looking forward to seeing Sarah and Lavender. As long as Dana and Chad had no idea where we were, it was all good. But we were all playing a dangerous game—Will and James included. We just had to cross our fingers that no one discovered what we were doing.

After all, no risk, no reward, right? We were up to our ears with the former, and with no guarantee of the latter, I wondered if we were all mad. With no other explanation forthcoming, I settled on that. We were a bunch of crazies about to gamble with our lives and livelihoods. Hopefully our odds were better than winning the lottery. If they weren't, well… it didn't bear thinking about.

CHAPTER 7

The next morning at 8:55 a.m., a knock sounded on the reception-room door. I opened it to Imani, Sarah, and Lavender while Abby wove around everyone's legs, and Ted barked excitedly. "You guys have great timing." I smiled and stepped aside so they could come in. We greeted each other with hugs and kisses on cheeks.

Lavender—his previously lavender hair now a deeper shade of purple—wore a pair of green jeans, black turtle-neck jumper, and golden-brown, hooded leather jacket. He bent to greet the animals, then straightened and looked at me. "We're definitely all in sync, darling." He stared at my face. "You're looking a little tired. Is everything okay?"

"Sleep is a sought-after commodity at the moment. There's so much going on that I can't turn my brain off. I end up lying awake until two most nights, and getting up early is killing me."

Imani laughed. "You call this early?"

I grinned. "You know it, lady."

Sarah frowned. "My brother's obviously not taking great care of you. I'll have to have a word."

"Oh, no, no, no, no! Will's been awesome, and he has enough going on right now. Come through so I can explain everything." We went into the living room and sat on the Chesterfields, Abby commandeering Sarah's lap, and Ted sitting at my feet. I filled them in—the witches, not the pets. Imani already knew everything, so she sat there and nodded or interjected with extra info every now and then.

Sarah looked dejected. "Oh, you're right. Poor Will."

Lavender, who was sitting next to me, grabbed my hand with both of his. "Don't worry, sweetie; we're here for you. To be honest, I'm kind of excited. I've been waiting for you to ask for my help again. I love the thrill of the chase. Helping catch criminals is fun!"

Sarah chuckled. "He keeps asking me to contact Will and put in our offer to help. If I'm honest, I enjoy it too. So any time you need us, just call. We're in."

I smiled. "Thank you two so much. It's awesome to have you on board. I'm just sorry the shopping is for show."

Lavender waggled his expertly manicured brows. "It doesn't have to be. We've got all day, sweetie."

"Well, first, you need to help Imani and I look different. We don't want to be spied by any PIB agents since I'm not allowed to be investigating anything, and she's supposed to be sick, or at least recovering from being healed."

Lavender released my hand and stood. He put his hands on his hips as he regarded Imani and me. Eventually, a self-satisfied smile slid onto his lips, and he nodded. "Mmmhmm, you ladies are going to look nothing like yourselves. This is going to be fun!"

Imani and I shared a worried look. He seemed altogether too happy about this. How much fun could it be to make disguises for people?

I soon found out.

I stared at Imani. She stared at me. We stood opposite each other in the middle of the living room. She wore a blue wig, the straight locks cascading to her waist. The sunglasses covering half her face were reminiscent of a Kardashian. He'd painted her lips and nails in bright-red lipstick. She wore tight black leather pants and a lipstick-pink shirt which was open to her ample bosoms, her cleavage squished together and heaving out for all the world to see. He'd at least given her a short black jacket with faux feathers at the collar. With her three-inch-heeled pink knee-high boots, she towered over me.

"Jesus," I said. Because, really, what else could I say.

She angled her chin down and looked at me over the top of her gargantuan eyewear. Rather than say anything, she burst out laughing. I sighed. I hadn't seen myself in the mirror yet. Lavender had magicked this stuff on me—it was real, but he didn't actually place any of it with his hands. Looking down at myself, I could see my tight dark blue jeans, which seemed to have, well, um, a bulge where there usually wasn't anything. "Oh my God. You can see everything!" I felt the outside of my jeans and tried to adjust things.

Everyone laughed. Sarah, tears streaming down her face, pointed at my crotch, then my chest. "Oh my God, Lily." That's all she managed before hugging her stomach and cackling some more.

I folded my arms. I was not amused. Needing to know how bad it was, I magicked my mirror from my bedroom to in front of me. It hovered just above the ground. "Seriously? Are you telling me there was nothing else you could have made me look like except a pimp or a sugar daddy?" My black shirt was open to just above my cleavage, which had been strapped down. Out of the open material curled dark chest hair, a thick gold chain tangled in its gross mass. "At least I'll be warm even with my shirt open." I raised an incensed brow. I carefully patted my combover with a flat palm. "This is so 2000s. Surely it would be hipper of me to shave my head at this point? And what's with this thin moustache?"

Imani gave one last snort and settled her laughter. "How do you think I feel, love? I have to be seen with you, like I'd date someone like that. Look at me. I'm a supermodel!"

"You totally are. You'd give Sarah a run for her money. You're both gorgeous." And I was right—in that getup, Imani looked like one hot woman. She normally downplayed her attributes, and I'd never seen her with so much make-up on. She was gorgeous, but this over-the-top getup gave her runway attitude.

Lavender nodded. "You so would. And that's the thinking behind my disguises for you ladies. You said you needed to take some photos on the way to the victim's home. We can hide in plain sight and pretend we're doing a grungy street-style photo shoot. You aren't her pimp or her sugar daddy, Lily. You're the photographer. I'm the make-up artist, of course, and Sarah is the stylist. We can have her fussing with necklaces and clothes."

I folded my arms and my gold bracelet—of course I was wearing one—got caught in my chest hair. "Son of a witch!"

Sarah grabbed my wrist. "Careful. You don't want to ruin the disguise." She managed to untangle everything.

When she was done, I tried folding my arms again, meticulously avoiding the dark thatch growing out of my shirt. "So, I'm a sleazy photographer? That's not realistic, is it?"

Sarah grinned. "Not normally, but I still come across them. Besides, the public will believe it. It's a cliché they know and love. I'm sure people will be too busy laughing at you to take too close a look."

"Are we ready to go, loves?"

I pouted. "No."

Sarah giggled. "Come on. You look nothing like you. Your disguise is perfect, and it is for a good cause."

She hit my empathy button—a sure-fire way to get me to go along with anything. "Yeah, yeah, okay." I magicked my Nikon and reflector to myself. At least I could get away with no tripod. Carrying too much stuff was a nightmare and one of the worst parts of the job if you had no assistant. "So, I guess we're not doing any shopping now."

Imani smiled. "There's no need. Lavender's done a top job. No one at the PIB could possibly tell who we are."

"Meow."

I looked down, and there was Abby. I bent and picked her up. "What's up?"

"Meow, meow."

Imani nodded. "She said be careful."

I rubbed my face against hers. "Thank you, sweetness. I will be." I kissed the top of her head and placed her back on the ground. "I guess it's time to go. The Mall Maidstone toilets, here we come." Hmm, didn't exactly have a heroic ring to it.

❧

When I exited the toilet cubicle, a middle-aged woman washing her hands took one look at me and screamed. What the hell? She finally found her words. "Get out!" She screeched at the top of her voice, "There's a man in here. There's a man!" Ooooooh, riiiiight. Oops. I held the top of my shirt together protectively.

Imani came out of the cubicle after me, and the woman's eyes opened wider, like an owl hyped up on fairy floss. Imani pushed my back, forcing me past the appalled woman. "Don't worry," she said. "It's my uncle. He's not too bright and needs help." The force on my back increased, hurrying me out of the toilets faster and into the main thoroughfare of the mall.

As the door shut, the woman screamed again, "They've been having sex in the toilets!"

Imani pulled me over to the side and kept her voice low. "Why did you go to the women's toilets? And where the hell is your no-notice spell?"

Whoops. "I didn't think I needed one. Wouldn't that draw attention if a witch saw us? Witches don't generally walk around with no-notice spells activated. Do they?" I looked over her shoulder, waiting for that woman to see us and be horrified all over again. "And I forgot I was dressed like this.

Sarah came out of the toilets, rubbing the back of the discombobulated woman. I hurriedly threw on a no-notice spell. "Honestly, I think we shouldn't have these up. It makes us look like we're trying to do something sneaky."

Imani regarded me, irritation emanating from her whole body. She folded her arms, making her cleavage pop out even more. A teenage boy walking past turned his head to cop a good look. He crashed into a young woman coming the other way. "Watch where you're going, tosser."

He blushed, then swore at her before hurrying on his way.

I looked at Imani's breasts. "Wow, those things even trump a no-notice spell. Who knew?"

She raised a warning brow. "Some are more easily able to see past our spells."

I smirked. "Mmmhmm. Cleavage, the great attention-grabber of all time. That's all I'm saying."

Sarah had finally convinced the woman that her life would be fine and that seeing a man in the women's toilets wasn't going to kill anyone and sent her on her way. Will's sister—dragging her small suitcase on wheels—joined our little group as Lavender came over. "Sorry I'm a minute late, ladies, but I couldn't help but give Ted and Abby some cuddles. They're adorable. I'm thinking I need a pet."

Imani looked at him. "Sorry to interrupt, but we're on a mission here. You can talk about pets when we're done." Imani nodded at me. "Lily's brought up an interesting point—we shouldn't wear no-notice spells because we don't care that people can see us, and it looks suss to any witches—they'll wonder why we're trying to fly under the radar."

Sarah grinned. "Great idea."

Lavender looked at me, clapped his hands together once, and laughed. "Oh, honey, too funny!"

"Nice rhyme." I couldn't resist pointing out the obvious, it was also a good way of changing the subject.

"Why, thank you." Lavender gave a small bow.

Sarah cocked her head to the side. "You need another name if we're dropping the spells. Frank should do it."

Being a Frank was the least of my worries, so there'd be no arguments from me. "Fine. Let's get out of here. I'll drop my no notice as soon as we're outside. If that woman's told any security guards, I don't want them figuring out I'm the guy." It would be just my luck to get arrested for indecency, then the PIB finding out because I'm a witch. Oh, how fantastically well that would go down with Chad.

Once outside, I dropped my no-notice spell, and Imani took the lead—as best she could on those ridiculous platforms. In fact, she was walking as fast as she normally did. Maybe they did special high-heel training at spy school. Goodness knew all the sassy women in thriller and spy films had to do everything in heels while their male counterparts got to wear flats. Maybe the men wanted an unfair advantage. I giggled to myself, and, for once, no one noticed. It was nice to remain unjudged for my sense of humour.

We made it to High Street and turned right. After a minute, I asked everyone to stop. I waved Sarah over and spoke quietly. "You're going to be my interpreter since I don't want everyone hearing that I have a woman's voice. It'll ruin my image." I grinned, and she giggled. "I'll get you to pass on the info as if I'm too important to relay messages."

She snorted. "Sounds good, sexy boss. What's your first message?"

"I want to take a couple of shots here, so I'll leave it to you as to how you want to say it. You know the fashion lingo."

"I'm not sure we have a lingo, but I'll do my best." She looked at Imani and Lavender. "Frank wants to stop here and take a couple of shots. We want some retail in the background, and later, we'll do grungy street shots in front of some houses. Capeesh?"

"Sounds fab, honey." Lavender looked at me. "Work your magic, Frankie baby."

I bit my tongue so I wouldn't laugh. I gave a chin tip and ran my fingers through my chest hair. My bracelet got caught again. "Ouch!"

Sarah spun around and untangled me. "Oh, Frank." She sighed. "How many times have I told you to be careful? What would you do without me?"

I lowered my voice. "I have no idea, but I'm going to kill Lavender later. I think I need to ditch this idiotic bracelet. Surely Frank can be uber cool without one?"

"Hmm, maybe."

"You're all so mean." I took off the lens cap, raised my camera, and handed my reflector to Sarah. "Here, you get to hold this. I'm sure you know where to put it."

"Ooh, Frank's getting all thingy. Don't worry; I'll do a good job." She placed Imani in the middle of the footpath, much to the annoyance of several pedestrians, if their cranky expressions were anything to go by. I lifted my camera and pointed it at her, the focus wide so I could get in as much of the street as possible. I whispered, "Show me Jasmine Harris the night she went missing."

Darkness descended. Goosebumps pebbled my arms and

the back of my neck. I shivered involuntarily. It was as if I was there… at night… alone. I forced my arms to keep the camera in front of my face when I'd rather lower it and escape the shadowed streetscape dimly lit with streetlights and the occasional neon sign.

Jasmine was there, her back to us, walking. I panned the camera around and behind me to see if anyone was following her.

"A bit of warning would be good, love. Honestly, bloody eccentric photographers."

I momentarily lowered the camera. Imani was shuffling as fast as she could on those monolithic platform shoes, trying to get in the shot. Oh, crap. I was about to apologise, then remember that I was an arrogant, abundantly chest-haired photographer. *You're Frank, not Lily.* I shook my head, disdain on my face. When I was done silently admonishing Imani, I lifted my camera again.

There was one guy further up, across the street, walking with hands in the pockets of a trench coat. His hat was drawn low, and the downward cast of his head meant his face was hidden—not that I could see much from this distance in the dark. On this side of the street, a couple walked holding hands. Considering the guy I'd seen with Lana Phillips had been wearing a similar hat, this was looking dodgy as.

I lowered my camera, enjoyed my brief reprieve into daylight, and waved Sarah over and pointed down the street. "I think I have something. Can you get Imani to walk further that way? This time, I'll photograph her facing me. Then I'll walk around and take a pic from behind. She can keep her back to me because it looks arty." I chuckled, even though cobwebs of unease clung from every nerve.

"Okay, boss. Are you all right? You look a little...."

"Jittery? Yes, but I'm fine. Job hazard."

"Are you sure?" Whilst we were keeping my talent a secret from as many people as possible, after Sarah's friend and then Sarah were kidnapped, and we needed Lavender's help to find them, Sarah and Lavender both found out about my photographic talent. They'd taken oaths not to tell anyone, plus I trusted them anyway. They were both awesome people who would never divulge my secret.

"Yep. Now, get along, or I'll have to fire you." I smirked. Trying to keep myself upbeat was a good idea. There was something about looking through my camera when it took me to another time. I wasn't sure if it was all in my head or if emotions came through, but it was almost as if I was there, and that could be freaky. It wouldn't be hard to get lost in the emotions and mire myself there all day. I had to be careful, and humour in this situation was my saviour. It was just lucky I was funny.

"I wish." She laughed and went to relay the information to Imani and Lavender. Without more fuss, Sarah handed Imani a hat and gold handbag—I guessed we needed to mix up the fashion stuff if we wanted to look legit—and they strode to our next "location" eighty feet away. I didn't want to go too far, in case I missed where our victim went. She could've crossed the road or ducked into another street, and I'd miss it and have to retrace my steps.

Once Imani was set up, pretending to hail a taxi, I pointed and called on my talent. Night-time closed in around me.

Jasmine was in the middle of the street, heading to the other side of the road. There was a side street close to her, and I'd say she was aiming for that. I clicked off a shot and lowered the camera. After positioning myself in front of Imani, I took a photo of the street behind her. The couple had stopped for a smooch. The guy in the trench coat was still walking towards Jasmine on the other side of the street. After clicking off a shot, I got out from behind my lens. I looked at my friends and jerked my head, indicating I wanted to cross the road.

We crossed, and I led them to the street I assumed she went into. A quick look through the lens showed I was correct. I walked a bit further and turned around. On a roll, I didn't want to wait for Imani to get into position. I pointed and asked my magic to show me the man who was following Jasmine. And there he was. But did my magic think he was just following her incidentally, or was it intentional? Time to be more specific. "Show me the man who snatched Jasmine."

Yep. He was still there. I lowered the camera and approached Imani, speaking to her quietly. "Can you stand where I put you? The guy is there, and I need to get some closeups."

"Sure thing, love." Her gaze shone with excitement, and was that a touch of awe? I guessed that before I came along, solving crimes took a lot longer. It was good to know when you were on the right track, and my talent was a fantastic indicator. I supposed my talent was awesome, but I wasn't going to confuse that with me. *I* wasn't my talent—I was just lucky to have it… or not. Seeing the things that I saw wasn't always the best fun ever.

I manoeuvred her to the spot he'd been in and stood two

feet away. Night fell again. I held my breath, fear telling me to stay silent. He was there, in front of me, face in shadow. His wide-brimmed hat prevented light from glancing his features. My heart raced as I took photos. *He's not really there. He's not really there.* I needed to stay my course. Maybe something would show up that I wasn't paying attention to right now.

I had a moment of reprieve as I walked around Imani, but then I was back in the darkness. *Click, click.* In the distance, over his shoulder, Jasmine continued her walk home. *Click, click.*

When I was done, we followed the path Jasmine had taken. Further along, she turned left into another dark street, walking past rows and rows of blind terraces, their lights out as the occupants slept, oblivious to the cat and mouse game unfurling outside. I didn't even think the mouse knew it was part of the game.

I stopped again and motioned for Imani to stand in front of me. Sarah gave her a red coat to put on, and Imani handed her the hat, then struck a pose.

"Show me Jasmine the night she was taken."

So, this was where it happened.

In front of a nondescript two-storey terrace home, he'd made his move. He gripped her upper arm, the glowing yellow outline of his doorway scoring the blackness. That was new. I'd never seen the actual magic in my camera before. Maybe it had always been there for me to see, but no one had made a doorway in the dark in one of my photos?

I lowered my camera, then said, "Show me that guy dragging her through his doorway." *Click, click.* I looked over the top of my camera. "This way." Imani let me guide her to the spot. "Thanks." I looked through the viewfinder again and took photos from as many angles as I could. If I went around the other side of the doorway, though, they weren't visible.

Jasmine's face was contorted in fear. Her hand was around the arm gripping her, and she was leaning away, as if struggling to break free. I couldn't see much of his face, just his mouth, which was curved up in the kind of smile you have when watching something amusing. Whatever he'd planned to do with her, he was definitely looking forward to it. My stomach somersaulted with her fear, and the image blurred as tears got in my way.

I clicked off numerous shots and lowered my camera. "Show me what happened ten seconds after he grabbed her." Well, there it was—an empty street. Considering how long ago it had happened, there was probably no magic signature left, but I asked anyway, quietly, of course, because in the daytime street, there was the occasional person walking past. "Imani, can you check the spot you're in for a magic signature?"

"Of course, love." Her magic tingled my scalp, stopping after about a minute. She shook her head. "Sorry, nothing. Can I see what you got?"

I nodded and handed her the camera. Sarah and Lavender crowded next to her on either side so they could have a look too. After scrolling through all the pictures, Imani looked up, her worried gaze meeting mine. Sarah and Lavender looked at each other, the seriousness of the situation piercing.

After a protracted silence, Imani was the first one to speak. "Let's head home."

We all nodded. There wasn't much else to say.

CHAPTER 8

Soon after arriving at Angelica's, Imani left, saying she was going to pretend to be a concerned friend and ask questions of the people living in the houses around where Jasmine disappeared. Sarah and Lavender stayed with me for the afternoon, tossing around ideas about what to do next. After they left, I snuggled on the couch with the fur babies and read. Even though we'd discovered something, it wasn't enough to take us much further with the investigation, and with Will's job on the line and Operation Food Poisoning, focussing was a problem. By the time Will got home at five—being desk-bound had some perks—I was exhausted.

As soon as I heard the reception-room door opening, I jumped up and ran, displacing two unhappy lap occupants. I got to the hallway as Will was shutting and locking the door. When he turned to face me, I gave him a huge hug. "How was today? Was it drama free?"

With one arm wrapped around my back, he stroked my

hair with the other hand. "Depends how you define drama. I had a boring day, but your brother went home vomiting. He'd given Beren the heads-up, so he made himself scarce, not to mention the healing would have taken the rest of the day and maybe the next to recover from anyway. Chad's secretary also went home ill. As soon as she did, Chad was calling around for an assistant. We made sure he got Liv."

"Oh my God, that couldn't have gone more perfectly! And to think we were so worried about getting her in there."

"It was about time something went our way, don't you think?"

I smiled. "Definitely. Come on, and I'll tell you about my day." We went into the living room and sat on one of the Chesterfields where Will greeted both animals. I supposed they figured I was coming back, clever furry people. Abby jumped onto his lap, and after getting a good pat, Ted sat at my feet. Such a homely, cosy scene. Who would've thought? If James had never gone missing all that time ago, I would likely still be living by myself in my Cronulla apartment, happy enough, but not nearly as happy as this. But, also, probably not nearly as stressed. Sometimes adversity led to something better. Who knew? Okay, so a lot of people knew, but it bared remembering, especially when things got difficult.

I relayed everything we'd done and what Imani had gone to do later. He nodded slowly. "Okay, that's a start. And you could only get a look at his mouth?"

"Yep. I suppose it's better than nothing."

"True." He stared at Abby for a moment, likely thinking, or was he talking to her? Gah, damn my lack of animal-communication skills. He finally looked up. "If only we knew where that doorway led. I think we need to go back to the church, see if you can get a picture of him taking her through his doorway too. It would at least establish a pattern."

"Okay. Can you get Imani to make another landing spot? After what happened with Piranha last time when she followed us...."

He pressed his lips together, and his brow furrowed. "I can't believe I didn't see how much of a psychopath she was." He shook his head and touched my cheek. "If anything ever happened to you...."

I shrugged. "Maybe you shouldn't bother about the handcuffs next time. This won't end while she's alive. I could see her managing to escape from prison or sicking one of her cronies onto us from there."

"Yeah, well, I won't be making that mistake twice. Whatever happens, it will be self-defence. There's no way she's coming anywhere near us without her power ready to go. It's her or you, and I'll pick you every time."

I knew he loved me, but getting that confirmation was comforting. "Well, that's a relief. Why do you think she picked now to attack us?"

He shook his head. "I have no idea. Grief over her boyfriend? Maybe something else is going on with RP?"

I'd asked this question before, but no one had managed to give me a definitive answer. And while this was just his opinion, I needed to talk about Piranha's accusation. Maybe talking about it would help me figure it out. "Do you think my mother killed hers?"

"I don't know. But does it matter? Whatever the reason, she's determined to kill you. If your mother killed hers, she would have done it for a good reason. That's all you have to know." He took my hand and squeezed it.

He was right. I wouldn't think any differently about my mother if she had—it would just be another motivation for Piranha's hatred of me. "Do you think she's more dangerous now?"

Deep lines scored his forehead. "Yes. That was a brazen attack in a crowded street in the middle of the day. She's definitely escalated things. We'll need to be extra careful from now on."

I gave a wry smile. "Even more careful? I'm not sure how that's possible." I was virtually a prisoner in my home, and I always had company whenever I went anywhere. We were also making sure we didn't go anywhere by traceable methods.

"We're beefing up security in the streets around the PIB, making surveillance of our staff harder, but where there's a will there's a way. I know her enough to know she's single-minded. When she wants something to happen, she'll make it happen, no matter the cost. We just need to be vigilant."

I took a deep breath. Tiredness sagged my shoulders and sapped me of enthusiasm. Living this way was exhausting. Would I ever be free? Gah, how depressing. I needed to stop talking about this. "I promise to be extra careful. Anyway, we still have that case to figure out. I'll call Imani, get her to come over so we can discuss it in person." Being secretive was hard work. Not being able to just call someone and spill everything was a pain in the behind.

"Sounds good. Now, if only we had a stronger lead on this guy. We're going to struggle with what we've got so far." And that was the depressing crux of it. Who the hell was this guy, and where was he going to strike next?

Unfortunately, I didn't have long to find out the answer to the second question.

Damn.

CHAPTER 9

The next morning, after taking more photos at the church and discovering our sicko had, indeed, taken the unconscious or dead Lana Phillips through his doorway, Imani, Will, and I returned to Angelica's for breakfast. Sitting around the kitchen table, coffee cradled in my hands, I sighed.

Will looked at me, concern shining from his eyes. "What's wrong?"

"I miss Angelica. As crabby as she sometimes is, she's family—the first person I knew from here." A sad smile found its way to my lips. "Even with all her crankiness and putdowns, at least she's honest—you know what you're getting. And at the heart of everything, she means well. She just wants us to be strong enough to survive. Gah, I hate that we can't do anything for her. I hope she's okay."

Imani cocked her head to the side, an understanding expression on her face. "I know, love. I'm worried too, but if anyone can come through difficulty, it's her. And now we've got Liv in the lion's den, maybe we'll get to the bottom of things before it's too late."

Will looked at me. "Let me ask you a question. When have we ever not gotten to the bottom of a crime?"

I couldn't help the smile that came. "Never?"

"Bingo!" He returned my smile. "If Angelica needs our help, we'll find a way to get it to her. We'll also get to the bottom of these missing-persons cases. He'll have made a mistake somewhere, or he will make a mistake, and we'll discover it. His days of kidnapping women will be over soon. And as for Dana, we're getting closer every day." Will's phone rang. "Agent Blakesley speaking." He listened for a minute. "Okay. Bye."

"Who was that?" I couldn't not know—it would bug me all day.

"Liv."

My eyes widened. "Is everything all right? They didn't figure out our ploy, did they?"

He slid a poker face in place. I bit my nail. "No, nothing like that. Chad's secretary is still off today, so Liv has one more day to dig, but something's happened." He looked at Imani. "Agent Alena Sorokina's gone missing. She had three days off, so it wasn't during work. Two nights ago, she went out with friends. Her mother raised the alarm when she didn't show up for their early morning walk today. I have to go in now. It's all hands on deck apparently."

Two divots appeared above the bridge of Imani's nose, and I rolled my eyes. "Gee, I'm surprised Chad cares. Isn't he trying to get rid of agents?"

"Her father's a good friend of the top PIB director and served the PIB for twenty-five years before he left us to set up his own security business." He stood and magicked his breakfast dishes clean and away. "Imani, I think you should have one more day off, see if there's anything you and Lily can figure out in our case. I'm not sure if I'll get any time to come back and update you, but if I do, I'll let you know."

I stood, gave him a hug and kiss goodbye. "Stay safe today."

He smiled. "Always." He turned to Imani. "See you later."

"Bye." After a couple of minutes, Imani's phone rang. "Damn. Looks like they're chasing me up too." She pouted, then answered. "Agent Jawara speaking." Whoever was on the other end of the line was brief. She hung up and frowned. "I'm sorry, Lily, but I have to go in—sick or not. They supposedly need me." She stood. "I'll let you know what happens. She could be missing for any number of reasons—angry ex, revenge from some criminal she's put away in the past, or...."

"Our guy?"

"Yep. I'll come by tonight, let you know what I find out. Who knows, we might need your help with this, Chad be damned. See you later, love."

I gave her a wave as she made her doorway. And then she was gone. I blew out a breath and looked down at Ted on the ground and Abby in the chair next to me—she was too good for the ground, apparently. "Looks like it's just me and you kids today." I stood and cleared the rest of the breakfast stuff away with a sweep of my arm—and I meant with magic, not by shoving everything onto the floor, although that would have been fun, and because of magic, easily cleaned up at the end.

I made my way to the living room and stared out the window at the garden and squirrels. If only I could go out there and play with the squirrels or go for a run. What an incredible thing it would be to be able to go wherever I wanted whenever I wanted without an escort. When all this was over, a tour of Europe, just me and my camera, and maybe the occasional Will, Liv, or Imani was in order. It wouldn't even have to cost that much. I could travel home most nights, maybe stay in hotels every now and then. There was no shortage of incredible things to capture in my camera. One day I'd have an exhibition. Hopefully that day would come before I was too old to enjoy it. At this rate, it felt like anything of that magnitude was a lifetime away.

Stop the pity party, Lily. I should listen to my own good advice —whining and feeling sorry for myself was the fastest way to achieve nothing good. A distraction was in order, so I magicked my iPad to myself—time to read.

Around lunchtime, my phone rang. "Tommy" came up on the screen. I ignored the little flutter of excitement that elicited and answered. "Hello, this is Lily."

"Hey, Lily, it's Tommy. How's it going?"

"Um, good thanks. How are you?"

"Really good. It's a madhouse here today. Apparently an agent's gone missing and they're pulling in all the agents to find her."

I didn't want to give away that Will told me things since most stuff would likely be confidential, so I pretended it was the first time I'd heard. "Wow, sounds serious."

"Yeah. Listen, I wanted to get out of this place for lunch. Can I interest you in meeting me for a bite to eat?"

"I'm sorry, but I'm housebound today." Gah, how embarrassing. How to explain it without telling him anything. I might as well make up a story. "My cat, Abby, is quite sick, and I don't want to leave her. Can we take a rain check?"

"Ah, yeah, sure. This isn't a fob off, is it?" He sounded dejected.

Guilt pounced on me. Poor guy. He didn't have any friends here. He must be so lonely, and he was cute. Unfortunately, if I left the house without an escort, there'd be hell to pay. I pushed away the desire to cheer him up and say yes. "No, not at all. Honestly, Abby's not well. Maybe another day? And we can invite Imani, too, since you don't know many people. She's an agent at the PIB, and she's really nice." Imani would probably give me grief for roping her into this, but too bad. This was a way to keep everybody happy and me out of trouble.

"Are you sure? I mean, I don't want to force you. You just seem so friendly, and I feel like we'd get along well. It doesn't hurt that you're gorgeous. Ah, sorry. Was that too much?"

I chuckled. And what were these hot cheeks? How embarrassing—blushing over a compliment from a guy... one who was *not* my boyfriend. *Get a grip, Lily.* "It's fine. I think you're nice too. I'll find out when Imani is available, and I'll text you. Is that okay?"

"Yes, sounds wonderful. Speak to you soon, gorgeous. Bye."

He didn't wait for me to say goodbye before hanging up. Okay, that was weird. I shook my head to clear it. Honestly, what was I doing flirting with him on the phone? I wasn't a cheater. How was it that I couldn't trust myself to have an above-board conversation with someone? If Will had heard, he'd be cranky, and rightly so. Maybe I shouldn't have lunch with him—Imani or no Imani. But then, I'd said I would, and I felt awful that he had no friends… plus, would it be that bad just to have one lunch? A quiet little voice inside me said, yes, it would be that bad, but I shut her up by getting back into my book. I didn't want that kind of negativity today.

At 6:00 p.m., Will came home, and James and Imani were with him. They strode into the living room with purpose, poker faces intact. I sat up, my veins pinging with nerves. The three of them in their uniforms with such cold expressions was intimidating. I automatically stood—maybe my subconscious felt safer without them towering over me. "What happened?" Had our scheme been discovered? Nausea swished in my stomach, and I placed my palm on it, trying to comfort myself. Abby headbutted the back of my leg, probably trying to give me some support. I thought a quiet "thank you" to her. Her purr was so loud, it was easily heard. Despite the wall of intense agents in front of me, I managed a smile, although it didn't last long.

James was the first one to break the silence. "We can't stay long, Lily, but we wanted to fill you in and make sure you were okay."

"What's wrong? Has something happened with Angelica?" My heart pounded, vibrating my chest and eardrums.

"No." James shared a glance with Will. What it meant I had no idea. "Alena's body has shown up. There was a spell on it, one her father put on her, that if anything should happen to her, and she died, her body would automatically transport to her parents' house."

My eyes bugged open. What the hell? How creepy but

clever. "Okay, but why are you all here looking like something major just happened? You never get so… weird and full on when it's any other PIB crime." My forehead scrunched. "Beren's not a suspect, is he?"

Imani's mouth dropped open. "Of course not. What the hell is going on in your brain, woman?"

"You're all so stressed. Can you just tell me before I freak out? The longer I wait, the worse my assumptions are."

James took over again. "She was in a state that indicated she'd been killed by a vampire witch."

I blinked, having no idea what that could mean. "Did they suck all her blood out? I thought vampires didn't exist."

Will shook his head. "They don't. It's a witch who drains another witch of all their power, killing them. It's like if you take in too much power, you can kill yourself. Vampire witches suck all the power out of another witch, drawing and drawing until they die. They're rare, though. Hundreds of years ago, the few vampire witches that existed were hunted and killed. There weren't supposed to be any, but sometimes old blood-lines can pop up, just like with genetic features in non-witches."

Their attitude still didn't make sense. "But that still doesn't explain why you're so worried. I mean, a normal witch could kill any one of us. Hell, Piranha almost killed us just yesterday."

Imani licked her bottom lip. "You don't understand, love. Their special talent is being a vampire, so they're equipped with things to aid them in that. The more power they take, the longer their life, and the more powerful they become. They inherit the talents of their victims for a year or two after they kill them. Part of their inherent talent is influencing. They're so subtle, you wouldn't even tell. If they want to spend time luring you in, they will. They could override the will of any of us. Before you realised what was happening, they'd have latched on, and that's the end of that. Once they're taking your power, it's too late."

Imani didn't know my other secret, the one about being able to use other witch's power. James had explained that it was dangerous because other witches would be scared of me. Did that mean I was a vampire witch? The skin in the middle of my back prickled, and my stomach dropped to the floor. Dizziness took hold, and I swayed.

James hurried to stand in front of me and grabbed my arms, carefully lowering me to sit on the couch. He sat next to me. "What's wrong?"

I stared into his eyes. "Does that make me one? I mean, you know…."

"No, Lily! You don't have the power of persuasion, and you only ever do it with the other person's permission. I don't know that you could force your way into another's power, and even if you could, that's it. You can't lure them. Your talent is dangerous, which is why we've kept it a secret, but if I thought for one minute you'd do it for the sake of it and force someone, I'd lock you up myself."

I swallowed and looked at Imani, whose eyes shone with curiosity. She didn't know about this secret, but maybe it was time. "But could someone else force me to steal someone else's power?"

Lines married his forehead. He looked up at Will and Imani, who both gave subtle shrugs. James looked back at me.

"I don't know. But let's assume they could. We just need to be very, very careful. And as far as every witch's safety, we need to be even more careful. This event even had Chad calling a truce for now. Will is back on agenting duties until we catch whoever is responsible."

The new information did not sit well with me, but through my panic, I still had a question. "What about a magic signature? Surely if he took all her power by force, he had to make a spell?"

James shook his head. "No. It's his talent. Seduction, mind control, he doesn't need spells. And the spell that transported her body home was made by her father, so we're getting nothing."

"Crap."

"Yes, Lily, that's about it," said Will.

I lifted Abby from her spot next to me and pulled her in for a cuddle. "So now what?" James, Will, and Imani shared a few looks. Silent intentions were flying all over the place, as if a pros-and-cons discussion was happening. "For God's sake, just tell me." Abby meowed, and I would bet she was backing me up.

Will held up his hands to my brother and Imani. "I'll ask, and I'll take the fall if anything happens. And before anyone argues, it's my choice, and I'm happy with it." When no one disagreed, his eyes met mine. "Lily, we need your help. The area where Alena's friends last saw her is swarming with agents right now, so we'll have to wait a day. But we think this might be the same guy, the one who's been taking the women."

"Wouldn't he take men too? Surely he wouldn't discriminate—a feed is a feed."

Imani came around and sat opposite James and me. "Not necessarily. If he's a straight male, flirting and seducing women would be more enjoyable, easier. He would potentially take men, but I would imagine that's only if a viable woman wasn't around."

"Okay, I can understand that, but what about the first victim. Wasn't she twenty-two? Did her magic come in early?" Witches got their magic at twenty-four, well, most of them— James had been an early bloomer.

Will sat next to Imani. "We're not sure because there hasn't been a vampire witch for a long time, but they may not need a witch who's come into their powers. They could potentially rip through the barrier that holds their powers at bay." He looked at James. "We'll ask Lana's family if she came into her powers early."

James nodded. "I'll get onto that tomorrow." James looked at me. "So, will you help?"

"I'm worried about you guys losing your jobs, but you've made your choice about it. Of course I'll help. And who knows? Maybe Chad will give you a pardon if he finds out, considering you're doing everything you can to find out what happened to this influential guy's daughter."

"Right." James stood. "When it's time to visit the site, I'll send Will to come get you. And before you ask, no, I don't know what time that will be. I'll see you all later. It's my turn to put my gorgeous daughter to bed tonight, and she's probably pretty hungry right now." We all said goodbye. Then he made his doorway and left.

Imani stared at me. "So, love, you're even more powerful than I thought. You can link with other witches and use their power?"

I shrugged, guilt at having kept a secret from her flushing my face. She was trustworthy—I mean… she'd sworn her life to protect me at great potential cost to herself. If I couldn't trust Imani, who could I trust? "Yes, but I can also give my power to someone else to use if I choose. I've only ever used it to save people." Was I a monster? Okay, so I'd done nothing with that ability except good, but what if it was a slippery slope?

Imani shook her head. "I can see the look on your face. You're not a vampire witch, love. I can promise you that. You don't have persuasion as a talent—how many times have you gotten into trouble for doing your own thing? If you had that talent, you'd get away with everything." She laughed. "Also, have you ever taken someone's power and stored it? Saved it for later?"

"Um… no. I just use it at the time. It's like I'm a fireman holding a hose. I just direct the flow—it comes through me, and I can do what I like with it, but I can't store it."

She sat back and smiled. "You're definitely not a vampire witch, then. They can store other people's power for one or two years, which also makes them extremely dangerous. They can offload a lot of power at once."

I'd be lying if I said that summation didn't have relief melting my bones. I exhaled a huge breath and sagged into the couch. I gave Imani a small smile. "Thanks for that. I feel a lot better now."

"Any time."

My relief, as usual, was short-lived. "Do you guys think he's doing this to stay young, or do you think he's saving the magic up to do something evil with?"

Will scratched his eyebrow. "Could be both. What I'm wondering is why Westerham, and where was he before?"

I had no idea how criminal minds worked, but I gave my opinion anyway because, well, I was me. "Maybe he's just moving his way across the countryside so no one gets too suspicious? One or two missing women in six months won't raise alarm bells, but six women in six months in similar circumstances would. How often do vampire witches need to feed, anyway?"

"Hmm. Hang on a minute." Imani's magic peppered my scalp, and a hardback leather-bound tome appeared on the low table between us. It was hefty—too big to have on a lap.

I sat forward and read the cover—*A Complete Guide to Vampire Witches: the dangers, skills, and desires of the witch world's most cunning predator.* "Catchy title." I chuckled because in what universe did I ever think I'd be reading out a title like that in seriousness. "That thing must weight twenty kilos."

Imani laughed. "Yeah, and it's not for lightweights." She drew on her magic again and put her palm on the cover. "How often do vampire witches need to feed?" She removed her hand, and the book opened, the yellowed pages flipping over almost too fast to follow. After a few seconds, it stopped, open at page 714. All of the first page and three-quarters of the second were in bold font.

"Is that the book highlighting what you wanted?" I asked.

She nodded. "Yep." She moved over on the couch so Will could shuffle closer to the book. They both leaned over it and read. Lazy me was just going to wait and see what they said. There was no need for all of us to read it.

"Hmm." Imani pointed to a paragraph. "Says here that witch vampires don't have to feed to survive but that they have a compulsion to—so an addiction, if you will. If they don't feed for a while, it's all they can think about until they do it."

Will's forehead wrinkled. "It also says down here"—he pointed to a paragraph at the bottom of the first page—"that they can feed without draining their victim, but they often get carried away in the euphoria of the *feed* and end up killing their prey."

"I suppose it's hard to eat just one piece of cake, especially if it's your favourite."

Imani and Will jerked their heads up to stare at me.

"What?" I thought it was a fairly accurate analogy. "Seriously, what's the problem?"

Will shook his head. "Sometimes I worry about you, Lily."

I laughed and shrugged. "Meh, whaddaya gonna do?"

Imani read more. "It also says that if they don't feed, rather than gain youth, they age quicker, but it's reversible if they feed enough."

"Are they immortal?" How amazing it would be to go out on your own terms, like if you get sick of things, you just let it go, but then does the need to feed overpower your desire to die? Is it immortality against your will?

Will shook his head. "Not that I've ever heard. Even though magic can keep you young, you still age, albeit at a much, much slower rate."

"How old do you think the oldest vampire was?"

"You're full of questions today, love. Hang on, and I'll see if I can find it." She placed her hand over the book. "How long can a vampire witch live?" The pages fanned the other way this time, stopping at page 307. Imani scanned the bold print—a small paragraph in the middle of one page. "The oldest recorded vampire was Marguerite Mercier, who died in 1642 aged 429." She looked up at me. "How true that is, though, who knows? Because of our magic, witches have managed to record more of their history than non-witches, but she could have lied. Unless someone fact-checked her age before she died by casting a truth spell on her, we can't know for sure."

Will looked at Imani. "Mind if I have a turn?"

She smiled. "Be my guest."

He hovered his hand over the tome. "How do you kill a vampire witch?" The pages flurried in a blur, stopping near the end of the book. After finding what he was looking for, he read, "'Killing a vampire witch may be the hardest task you will ever face, but know that it is not impossible. Many vampire witches were killed during the great cleanse of 1685-92. Before destroying a vampire witch, he must be stricken unconscious; otherwise, he will overcome his attacker with his strength of both magic and persuasion.'" Will cleared his throat, then magicked himself a glass of water. After having a sip, he continued, "'Once without his faculties, he is ripe for the killing. A talisman of intensification will be needed, for even without his wits, his talent will fight back to save itself from destruction.'"

My mouth fell open, and adrenaline shot through me. "What? They fight back even if they're out of it? How the hell is anyone going to kill it, because we clearly need to. There's too much risk he could talk his way out of jail and keep killing. Do we even have a talisman of intensification?"

Will's shoulders sagged. "Nope, we don't have one. And the protocol has always been to kill them. Not sure how modern witch laws want us to deal with it. If he were any other type of criminal, we'd arrest him. I think we need to risk getting some cuffs on this guy and think about the rest later." He looked back down at the page. "If we did have to kill him, it says 'using the talisman of intensification, the attacking witch must send all their power to the vampire witch's magic centre until the body bursts into flames, turning them to ash.'"

Imani blinked. "That's dramatic. So, who's volunteering?" Her deadpan expression gave nothing away. Was she scared or confident? "If we couldn't render the vampire witch uncon-scious, *would* our handcuffs even work?" Yikes. If they didn't work for whatever reason, Will's idea to cuff him was toast. "I'll ask the book." Imani waved her hand over the pages and asked. Nothing happened, and all the bold highlighted words faded to normal font.

It didn't seem as though it was all doom and gloom. "The book didn't say the cuffs wouldn't work. Whenever it was magicked together, there probably were no magic-blocking handcuffs."

"You're right." Will sat back. "It's better than a no, at least."

"Agreed," said Imani. She looked back at the book. "Can vampire witches feed from immature witches?" I suppressed a chuckle. That would rule out feeding from me then. "Here we are. 'Vampire witches can break through the barrier of a witch who hasn't come into their powers, however, the flow will be more of a trickle and, as such, they are unlikely to bother.' So, that answers that." She looked at her phone. "It's getting late. I suppose I'd better be getting home for dinner."

I shared a quick look with Will—he knew what I was suggesting. I turned to Imani. "Stay, have dinner here. We're going to get Indian delivered. Come on. I know it's one of your faves."

"Are you sure I'm not intruding?" She waggled her brows.

I laughed. "It's fine. I'll have my way with him later."

She laughed too. "Okay, fine. You've twisted my arm." She looked at Will and jerked her head towards the book. "Are we finished with this?"

"That's a yes from me."

Imani nodded and waved her arm. The foremost and heaviest authority on vampires disappeared, but my misgivings hadn't. How were we going to find this vampire let alone catch and trap or kill him before he moved on? And with one of the PIB agents a victim, would he strike close to home again soon? It looked as if his last three victims were from Westerham. Were there more we didn't know about?

There were so many questions we didn't have answers to. But fortified with beef vindaloo, I vowed to find them, and hopefully, the only one getting burnt would be the vampire witch.

CHAPTER 10

The next morning, I woke up late—not falling asleep until almost 2:00 a.m. would do that to a person. Will was long gone to work, so I ambled down to the kitchen. I magicked the fur kids their breakfast, then sat at the table to enjoy my cappuccino. It was about time for a visit to Costa. I hadn't been for a few days, and I was having double-chocolate-muffin withdrawals. If only that were my biggest problem.

I magicked my phone to myself from upstairs and turned the ringer up. I always put it on silent when I went to bed, for obvious reasons. There was one message. My friend Michelle, from Sydney, had texted to touch base. I pouted. When would I get back and see her? Would I ever? I swallowed—that thought scared me more than I cared to think about. A few weeks after I decided I'd be staying here, I'd arranged to have my possessions moved to a storage facility, and I'd employed a real-estate agent to rent my unit out. I hoped the tenants were taking good care of it. As much as I loved England, and I had a lot of unfinished business here, I did want to go back one day, maybe take Will and show him where I grew up. It really was a beautiful part of the world I was sure he'd love.

I replied to Michelle's message and put the phone on the table. I tipped my head back and stared at the immaculate white ceiling. No inspiration or comfort there. Waiting sucked. Gah. I finished my coffee and magicked the cup clean and away. Standing, I sighed. What to do today to fill in the time? It felt like I was wasting my life sitting around doing nothing. If it wasn't for RP, I could've popped over to France or Germany or Switzerland and taken some stunning photos. Instead, I was stuck here waiting for someone to show up and give me something useful to do.

My phone dinged with another text. Wow, Michelle was up late. I picked my phone up. My heart beat faster. It was Tommy. Crap. What did he want now? I mean, it's not like I didn't want to hear from him, but Will would not be happy I was texting another guy who wasn't James or Beren… or Lavender, for that matter. I opened the message.

Can you do lunch today? If not, no matter. We can maybe catch up another day.

Yes, I had time, but there was no way I was leaving this house without permission, and there was no way Will would say yes if I told him who I wanted to have lunch with. *I'm sorry. Today is not a great day. Maybe next week? I'll text you.* Gah, why did I say that? Maybe I could explain to Will that I felt sorry for Tommy, and we could all have lunch with him. I just didn't need to tell Tommy everyone else was coming. Why was life so hard?

Okay, Lily. I'll hold you to that. Have a lovely day, gorgeous x.

I sucked in a breath. What the hell? Oh my God. If Will saw that, I'd be in so much trouble. I wasn't even going to respond. Actually, I'd go one better. I deleted the whole conversation. If it didn't exist, I didn't have to deal with it. It wasn't like I did anything wrong. I didn't message him first or flirt that time. Nope.

"Hey."

I jumped, flinging my phone into the air. It flew across the room and slammed into the splashback before thunking onto the countertop. I spun around, out of breath. "Jeeze, Will. What the hell? You scared the crap out of me."

He raised a brow and stared at me, then narrowed his eyes. "You have the look of a guilty person."

I shook my head. "No. Not guilty of anything. You just surprised me, and you know how much I love those."

He turned his head slightly and gave me a side-eyed look before giving in. "Fair enough. Sorry. You just have that look, you know? And your cheeks are flushed as if you've been naughty."

I laughed. Hopefully it didn't come out as nervous. "It's been a while since someone's called me naughty." I waggled my brows.

Will stepped forward and looked down at me. "Are we good?"

I gave him my most sincere look. "Of course we are. I love you." I tilted my face up for a kiss, which he readily gave. Time to forget Tommy existed. I'd deal with that later. With a vampire witch on the loose and Dana's dad's warehouse thing tomorrow night, I had enough trouble coming my way. "Is it time to investigate?"

"Yes. It's a lot earlier than I thought, but our agents have done a thorough search of the location, and they've left. They're spending the day interviewing her family and friends, chasing up any enemies she or her father might have, seeing if there are any violent exes in the mix, etcetera, etcetera. I've had Imani set up a landing spot for us. I'll take you there. Then I'll let you do your thing and watch from afar. I don't think any agents will be lingering, but you never know. The average agent may not notice who you are, but they'll recognise me. Is that okay?"

"Of course it is. I trust your judgement. You're the spy person, not me. If I wander off while I'm taking the photos, it's because I might have a lead. Okay?"

"Roger that." Will made a doorway. I magicked my camera to myself, donned a return to sender, and stepped through. "Oh, wow." I shuffled forward, giving Will room to come through. "You could've warned me." We'd landed in a posh living room with large multi-paned windows. A crystal vase sat on a white mantel, which framed a fireplace. A plush sofa and two designer-looking chairs sat around a Persian rug. "I take it the PIB owns this place?"

"Yep. It's a two-bedroom apartment one of the high-level agents lives in as part of their remuneration. He gave us permission to put a doorway spot here. It's not often we can use our properties, but we were just lucky that the last time Alena was seen alive was just outside. Come on."

We stepped outside onto the footpath. I kept my voice down because someone might think I was nuts. "Where are we?"

"Notting Hill."

"Ooh, like in the movie. What was it called? You know… the one with Hugh Grant."

Will looked at me as if I were an idiot. He snickered. "*Notting Hill.*"

I snorted at my stupidity. At least I could laugh at myself. "Oh, yeah." There went my memory, making a fool of me yet again. Oh, well, nobody was perfect. "So, where am I looking, exactly?"

Will walked along the footpath for a minute; then we crossed another street. The buildings were mostly white rendered-brick four-storey character apartment buildings from what I could tell. We stopped across the road from a three-storey brownish-brick building with white archways above the windows. "Core by Clare Smyth. Is that a nightclub?"

"It's a posh restaurant."

"So, Alena was living large?"

"Her father's mega wealthy, so I suppose that's how she rolls."

"Why do they call it 'the other half?' It's not like half of the people can afford this. They should call it the other 1 percent."

"Yes, they should, but, Lily, we're not here for social commentary." He scratched his cheek. "She was last seen over there." He raised his chin, indicating far down the street. "She walked down there and turned right, and that was the last her friends saw of her. They'd stayed here chatting while they waited for their Uber."

I bit my lip as I gauged the distance. It was a fair way, but RP couldn't follow me now, and we'd gone via a doorway, so it was virtually impossible that they'd know where I was. "Okay. I'll be back in five. If I do have to wander further away, I'll give you a wave."

"Okay. Be careful. I'll be watching." He smiled.

I crossed the road and hurried along the footpath, craning my neck every now and then to make sure I wasn't being followed. I stopped about thirty feet before the intersection so I could get a picture of her at the corner. "Show me Alena the last time she was here." Headlights shone through the darkness from across the intersection, silhouetting the tall, slim woman who was dressed in a dark coat and what looked like pants and flat boots. I blinked and sucked in a breath. The car was moving, coming towards me. I'd lucked into a video. This had only happened a couple of times. Adrenaline burned swiftly through me. What would I be shown? The buzz was equal parts excitement and fear. I pressed Record. Yikes, I'd almost forgotten to.

She turned left around the corner. I jogged after her, the image bouncing around. As soon as I rounded the corner, she was in sight, so I walked again. Remembering that I was actually in another time, I risked a glance over the top of my camera so I wouldn't crash into anyone. The Nikon screen played the video as I walked, so it seemed that I could do both —watch where I was going and use my talent. Awesome.

A car cut across the centre line and pulled up next to her, facing the wrong way to the rest of the traffic. The driver must have beeped because she stopped and turned. The driver door opened, and someone leaned out… someone wearing a wide-brimmed hat. I ran to get around and in front of her so I could see who it was, but before I could get there, he'd shut his door, and she was walking around to hop into the passenger side. *Don't get in. Dammit!* I wanted to scream the words, but I was a day or two too late.

More frustration was in order—I couldn't film the man's face because he'd turned to look at her as she slid into the car, and the brim of his hat covered what I wanted to see. Damn.

I panned down to get the number plate, but there wasn't one. For goodness' sake. This guy had all his bases covered, but it looked to be someone she knew, otherwise why would she get in? She would've known he was a witch, so not a non-witch she stood a chance against.

The car took off and veered back onto the correct side of the road. And that was it. I filmed until their lights disappeared. Other than the vampire witch, I was the last one to see her alive. A shiver skimmed my spine.

I stopped recording and turned at heavy footsteps. Will ran towards me, then stopped in front of me, his thick, wavy hair dishevelled. "What the hell, Lily? You didn't wave."

"Oops, sorry. I got carried away because I got a video. But you saw me anyway. Does it really matter?"

"We agreed."

"Yes, but the outcome is the same. You knew what I was doing because you were watching."

He huffed. "Fine. So, what did you get?"

I handed the camera to him. When he finished watching it, he handed it back. "Let's head home and watch it again. I'll call James and Imani. Let's put this on your laptop, see if we can see anything when it's bigger."

"Unfortunately, I had to watch it on the screen mostly because I was hurrying, and I didn't want to trip or smash into someone." As I spoke, three people walked past. "Case in point."

"Hang on just a sec." His magic tingled my scalp. After a minute, it dissipated. He frowned and shook his head.

"No signature?"

"No. Come on. I'll go first, just in case. Stay a bit behind me." We headed back to the apartment, and soon we were home, James and Imani waiting for us in the reception room. I unlocked the door, and we went through to the living area, Will sitting next to me on one Chesterfield, James and Imani sitting on the other. Will magicked his laptop onto the table and opened it. He took my camera and hooked it up, then played the footage.

Imani was the first to give her opinion. "She looks happy to see whoever it is, doesn't she?"

James sat back. "Yep. Looks like she knows him and definitely trusts him."

Will shook his head. "Or his talent at persuasion was just too strong. With all her training, he still bamboozled her. This just proves how dangerous he is."

Imani sighed. "No number plate. Still, I'll run the car make and model through the system, see if anyone's reported one missing in London."

"Um, mind if I make a suggestion?" Something just occurred to me, and I didn't know why no one had already thought of it.

James nodded. "Of course. Go ahead."

"Why don't we drive out there and I see if I can get another movie happening and follow the car? I mean, if it ends up being photos only, it'll be painful but not impossible. We can see where they ended up."

Will's brow scrunched. "That will use so much power, Lily. And if we're driving from somewhere, we risk RP following us. Are you sure?"

I shrugged. "We have no other leads, do we? Besides, since I haven't actually got a job, I can sleep all the next day if I have to. We could go back there now if you like?"

Will and James shared one of their hard-to-decipher looks. Then James spoke. "We've got the warehouse gig tomorrow night, so if we could get this thing sorted today, I'd prefer it, but if it leads nowhere, we all need to mentally prepare for tomorrow night. We can't go into this distracted."

"Hang on a minute." Will opened the Google bar on his computer and looked up car-hire places. "There's one here, about five minutes from Notting Hill, and there's a convenient landing spot within a couple of blocks. That makes it a tad safer. We'll keep you updated."

James stood. "I have to get back to HQ, but, Imani, you go with them. If anything happens, better three of you than two."

We didn't muck around. It took us ten minutes to travel to a public toilet, walk to the car-hire place, hire a car, and drive to where I'd last seen Alena. Will was driving. I was in the front so I could film, hopefully, and Imani was in the back paying attention to the world around us—a lookout.

Looking through my viewfinder so I got the full experience,

I crossed my toes—my fingers were busy—and pressed Record. "Show me Alena driving away with the man who killed her." Headlights beamed out of the night, and they were moving! "Woohoo!"

Imani chuckled. "Video working, I take it?"

"Yep."

"Don't forget to direct me, and try not to leave everything until the last minute. I don't want to have an accident."

"Not a prob." The car continued down the road, and about two minutes later, I said, "Turn left." After fifteen minutes and a few more turns, the car pulled into a driveway outside a two-storey terrace. "Stop!"

Will slammed on the brakes, and I shot forward, my seat belt jerking me back into my seat.

"Lily!" Will gave me a dirty look.

"Sorry." I put my eye back to the viewfinder. The Vampire Witch opened the door for his victim and held her hand. He took her to the front door, unlocked it, and they went inside. "Oh my God." I stopped recording. "They went into that house just there. Number thirty-two."

A car beeped. Will glanced into his rear-view mirror. "Hang on a minute." He found a place to park a few doors up —it was our lucky day. London parking was a disaster at the best of times. Once the car was turned off, he held his hand out. Imani unclicked her belt and shuffled forward, a hand on each of our seats while she looked over Will's shoulder. They watched the last minute of footage. Then they watched it again. "She's definitely not scared of him."

"You got that right," said Imani. She turned her head. "What number was it?"

"Thirty-two. What street are we in?"

Imani looked on her phone. "Hanover Road."

"I'll call it in." Will dialled headquarters. "Hey, Liv. How's it going? Yeah… okay. Yep. 32 Hanover Road, London. Can you look up who owns the property and check that it's owner-occupied? Thanks…. ASAP. Sorry. Thanks. Bye." Will hung up and turned to me, then twisted around to look at Imani. "Now, we wait."

I turned my head and peered down the street a bit, to the pleasant-enough looking home. At least there wasn't a car there now, so the coast was clear if we wanted to get out and have a quick look. Was that the house of a killer? Were the other women buried in the backyard, or had he magicked their bodies somewhere? My eyes widened. "What if those two women are still alive, and he's been feeding off them all this time?"

Will's tone was gentle yet firm. "If one of the women died, chances are he's killed the others too. I also don't think that he'd be out risking himself taking another woman if he already has one… or two at home to feed off. He doesn't need to feed often, don't forget."

"Maybe he's cocky and arrogant?" It might be stupid of me, but I had to hold out at least a little bit of hope we'd get to one of the women in time.

Imani leaned forward into my space. "Or he enjoys using his talent and gets off on dominating and taking what he wants."

Will's phone rang. He answered it. "Hey, what's up?" He stared out of the windscreen as he listened. "Right. Okay. Thanks…. Just waiting on Liv to get back to me about something. I might have a lead." James's voice came through, but too muffled to understand as the phone was jammed against Will's ear rather than on speaker. Will nodded at whatever he said. "Yep. Okay. Bye." He hung up and turned to Imani and me. "We've just had confirmation that Lana Phillips's power came in early. She got her power at twenty-one, and she was strong, apparently."

"Is there like a scale you can measure witches by? Like an IQ test but for magic?" It seemed this should be a thing.

Will studied my face. "No, but you make a good point. It's usually just the people around you can feel your power when you use it, and it's a rough judgement. You know you can feel the range of power when someone's using, can't you?"

"Yeah, I suppose so." Now that I thought about it, he was right.

Imani sat back in her seat. "Some witches are better at feeling the level of other witch's power though. It doesn't really matter for everyday stuff. A small level of power is adequate to cook, clean, and travel. So no one worries about how strong they are. It's when you get to law enforcement or maybe a job where you're using your power as a skill that it matters. It's not like the general witch public are out there shooting lightning bolts at each other."

Will nodded. "It also matters in crime syndicates, but let's not get into that right now. The point is, he's targeting strong witches because they would have more power to give him, and I know Alena was one of our best."

Hmm. "How is he finding them?"

Imani said, "Randomly. Like a spider. He puts out his web —an ad on a dating site for instance—and waits. He might have ten dates before he finds someone worth draining. Maybe he hangs outside witch nightclubs too. I would imagine part of his talent is that he can tell how strong witches are just by looking at their aura."

I nodded. "Makes sense. So he's opportunistic as well as setting 'traps.'"

"I'd imagine so, love."

Will's phone rang again. "Hey, Liv. Yes. Okay…. Mmhmm…. Can you text it to me? Great. You're a gem. Thanks." He hung up. "We've got the owner's name, but it looks as if he rents it out as an Airbnb. We'll pay him a visit. He's not a witch, by the way, so don't let anything slip." He raised a brow at me.

"I'm offended by that suggestion. I don't let things slip. Besides, you're the agent, not me. I'm happy to sit in the car and wait for you to get back."

Will twisted around to look at Imani. "What do you say? I'll go get the information, and you can stay here with this one."

Imani smiled. "Sounds good to me."

Will shut his eyes, and his magic tingled my scalp. After a minute, he opened his eyes. He smiled. "I can see by your face that you have no idea what I just did."

"Maybe. And why does that make you so happy? No wonder you're a spy—you love having secrets." I chuckled.

"Maybe." He waggled his eyebrows. "I was consulting the magic map and finding the nearest public toilet I could use. There's one a couple of minutes' drive from here. Let's go."

While Will used the Roundwood Park toilet, Imani and I took a walk around the adjoining park. Ten minutes of fresh air and we were back in the car, Will full of information. "It was a weekend booking from a Mr Simon Parks. I have his bank details, but his profile on Airbnb has been deleted, funnily enough. I would imagine any personal information he gave is all fake anyway."

I sighed. "I suppose his name is fake too?"

"Most likely. I've texted Liv and asked her to look it up. In the meantime, we have the owner's permission to enter the property as he has no guests for three more days." He held up a key and smiled.

Imani grinned. "Nice work, Agent Blakesley."

"As always." He winked.

I rolled my eyes. "Okay, genius crime fighter, let's go."

This time, we parked in the car space the vampire witch parked in not long ago. As I exited the car and shut the door, goosebumps skittered up my arms, and I shuddered. Were we catching up with him, or would he disappear to another city, even another country before we could pounce?

Will led the way to the front door and unlocked it. Inside the narrow white-painted, timber-floored hallway, I readied my camera. "Show me the vampire witch last time he was here with Alena." Nothing. I wandered through the first door on the left, into a bedroom. There was no video this time; instead, it was a still shot of the vampire witch kissing his victim on the mouth, one hand cupping one side of her face, the other low on her back. He was still wearing his hat, for goodness' sake. Why couldn't he have made my life easier and ditched the hat once he was inside? Maybe he was going bald and was touchy about it? Nah, being a witch, he could grow himself some hair, couldn't he? Or at least stick some on magically. *Oh my God, Lily, this stuff is not important.* Focus.

I clicked off some shots, then asked my talent for more evidence. Nothing happened. "My magic's snubbed me. This is all I could get." I showed Will and Imani the pictures.

Will cocked his head to the side. "Hmm. At least he's left lots of DNA behind."

Imani frowned. "Yeah, but if it's not in the system, that's only going to help if we manage to get him to trial."

I looked more closely at one of the photos. "He's also wearing a distinctive ring on his middle finger. See there." I magnified the photo on the camera screen. The middle finger of the hand on her back wore a thick gold band with three lines of blue stones cutting diagonally across the top.

"Good pick up, love. The only problem is that we can never show these photos to anyone."

I sighed. "At least *we'll* know. I'm sure if we ever find this guy and arrest him, we can figure out an excuse then."

Imani nodded. "Agreed. We need to get this guy off the streets. None of us are safe while he's around."

Will gazed around the room. "I'm just going to look for a magic signature. Imani, can you do a sweep for physical evidence? If there's anything that looks out of place, let me know. I'd say strip the bed, but the whole place has been cleaned and the linen changed since they were here."

"Can do." Imani pulled out her phone and took a few normal photos. Then she knelt and looked under the bed. After that, she made her way around the room and out to the rest of the house.

"I'll have a wander, too, see if anything else shows up in my camera." I did a lap of the home and found nothing else. He likely killed her in that room in the morning, and she instantly went back to her parents' place. Had she been scared when he'd started draining her, or did his magic overpower that awareness? In normal vampire stories, the victim was supposedly in ecstasy, so they didn't care. I just hoped her last hours weren't terrifying.

Once we were done, we hopped back in the car and returned it. I travelled home, and Will and Imani went back to headquarters. I had no idea how what we'd found would help discover who the guy was. We had no magic signature and no face. Why did this have to be so hard?

My phone rang—Millicent's name on the screen. "Hey, Mill. How's it going?"

"Good. Just wanted to make sure you knew we're still having *dinner* at ours tomorrow night."

"Ah, yes. I know you guys are busy at work, so I wasn't sure if you'd want to postpone it."

"Nope. It's the best night for us, so we'll go ahead."

"Cool. I'll be at your place at seven. See you then."

"Bye, Lily."

Okay, so add that to my worries. Thanks, universe.

I decided to spend time reading—my great escape. Any excuse to cuddle up with my fur babies was welcome. After a couple of hours, I looked up. It was dark outside. I checked my phone. Five thirty. I didn't usually bug Will at work, but I felt like company… well, human company, so I texted him. *Do you know what time you'll be home? Thought I'd make pasta marinara for dinner.*

He didn't respond for five minutes, which felt like an hour.

Sorry, hon. I'm going to be here till late. I'll see if Imani wants to come over. I think she's almost done. Love you xx.

Okay. Miss you. Love you too xx.

My phone rang. "Hey, Imani. Did you speak to Will?"

"I sure did. He asked if I wanted to come over for dinner, but I thought maybe you'd like to go out for a change. I can meet you at the place rather than drive and give ourselves away. There's a lovely Italian at Maidstone—La Viletta. I can meet you at The Mall toilets—the same ones we used the other day."

Mmm, I could practically smell the garlic bread. "I'm in. Is Will okay with me going out?"

"He said it's fine because we're not driving. No one should know where you are."

"Cool. What time do you want to meet?"

"In an hour, so six thirty?"

"Done. See you soon. And thanks." I smiled, even though she couldn't see it.

"My pleasure, love. Looking forward to it. Ciao."

"Bye." I did a little happy dance while sitting by bouncing my legs up and down and waving my arms. Silly, I knew, but it was rare I got to go out to dinner. Being cooped up was enough to get anyone down. Instead of feeling like the twenty-four-year-old I was, I often felt like I was seventy. Actually, a seventy-year-old probably had a better nocturnal social life than I did. Whenever I caught up with people, it was usually to investigate a crime. Gah, how sad. Well, I didn't have to be sad tonight. I grinned and figured out what to wear.

At six thirty, I dressed in tight black jeans, black knee-high mid-heeled boots, a shiny red shirt, and red coat—I'd treated myself a couple of weeks ago. I figured having one coat when I lived in a freezing climate was ridiculous. In Sydney, I hardly ever needed a coat, so I'd only had one, and that had been for emergencies. I checked myself out in the mirror, loving how vibrant the outfit was. I put on some red lippy to match and was ready to roll. I brought up the coordinates for The Mall and made my doorway.

Imani wasn't hanging out in the toilets, which was probably a good thing, so I headed straight out into the main shopping centre. Just as I got outside, my phone dinged. *Lily, I'm so sorry, an emergency came up. I'll be about fifteen minutes late. Tommy volunteered to keep you company till I get there, and Will thought it was a good idea too. See you soon xx.*

I frowned. This wasn't a good start to my night out at all. If only they knew I'd been trying to avoid Tommy because he was too attractive for my own good. This could be a total disaster. *Okay, Imani, just get here as soon as you can. I'm hungry lol.* That didn't sound desperate for the wrong reasons, and it was true—my stomach grumbled to prove my point.

"Lily!"

Sigh. I recognised that male voice. I pretended it didn't create butterflies in my stomach. I turned around. "Hey, Tommy. Thanks for filling in for Imani. You know that I'm okay waiting by myself though."

He smiled, his blue eyes sparkling. His teeth were so perfect, it was as if I were watching a toothpaste commercial. *Think Will thoughts.* "I know, but I've been trying to pin you down for a while now. As soon as Agent Jawara asked, I wasn't going to say no. Plus, I feel better knowing you're safe. That vampire witch is out there somewhere. Everyone at work is talking about it. You never know when he'll show up."

I shivered. "Yeah, I suppose you're right. Why don't we find a chair and sit while we wait?"

"We can go to the restaurant if you like… have a drink."

At least it was a public place. I shrugged. "Sounds fine. I'll just text Imani." I sent her a text telling her I'd meet her at the restaurant. "Okay, let's go. Oh, I don't even know where it is."

He smiled. "Agent Jawara explained it to me, and I have it on my phone map. This way, my lady." He bowed. I giggled, but what I really wanted to do was tell him to stop being so adorable and that I loved Will. Funnily enough, nothing came out of my mouth. I was such a traitor. I should slap myself across the face. I lifted my hand and looked at it. Should I, or shouldn't I? "Lily, hello. Are you all right?" Tommy peered at me, concern on his gorgeous face.

I lowered my hand, disappointed in myself. "Um, yes, all good. I have moments of zoning out, so don't worry." I gave him a smile. "Lead the way."

He grabbed my hand and headed for the doors. A tingle zapped up my arm. Crap. He. Was. Holding. My. Hand. I should remove it. But what if I offended him? And it was kind of nice. *No, Lily, stop holding it.* But it wasn't like I'd kissed him or anything. *What a slippery slope, Lily. Imagine if you—*

"Earth to Lily. You're taking the challenge out of it."

Huh? "What?" My mouth dropped open. Instead of walking out into the partly illuminated night-time of Maidstone town centre, we were in a… bedroom. What the hell?

"You should pay more attention. It's cute though. You're actually gorgeous too. Maybe I'll play with you for a few days before I drain you completely." My brain foggy, it took a moment for it all to sink in. The clincher was the golden ring on the black bedside table. He pushed me against the wall and kissed me.

I wanted to fight, but as soon as the idea formed, it dissipated. I couldn't control my thoughts, turn them into actions. And the warmth on my lips travelled deeper, to my stomach. Was he drawing my magic already? I briefly came back to myself. I was kissing him back. Noooooooooo! *Resist, Lily*. But my body didn't want to resist; it wanted to kiss Tommy and get lost in him. The little piece of my brain that was cowering and watching with horror needed to think fast.

He finally stopped kissing me. "You know why I came here?"

"To your bedroom?" Gah, what a stupid question. Why wasn't I telling him I didn't care, that he was a murdering bastard?

He chuckled. "No, to Westerham."

"Um, why?" I looked at his lips and hoped he'd kiss me again.

His sly smile told me that he knew what I was thinking, and he took great pride and satisfaction in having totally conquered my will. "I heard through the grapevine that there was a powerful little witch. Don't look so surprised—witches talk. If you think you've been under the radar, think again. As soon as I laid eyes on you, I knew you were the one I had to have."

"Why wait so long to come get me, then? Why kill those other women first?" I blinked, surprised at the fairly rational question.

He cocked his head to the side, likely thinking. "Hmm, anticipation? I like to work up to my targets. Those other women were an entrée, side dish, and main course, if you like. But you are the crowning glory, the piece de resistance, dessert. He smiled and stroked my cheek with his nose. I took a breath and tried to think. He wasn't draining my power at the moment, and there was nothing stopping me from pushing him away. So why didn't I? He leaned back and gazed at my face. "You like me. That's why you don't run. We're meant to be together, Lily, even if it's only for a few days." He chuckled. "Even if you wanted to leave, you couldn't—I've warded my house against it." He stroked my hair. "Once you're dead, I'll always carry a little bit of you with me, a tiny sliver of magic tucked away so I never forget what you gave me."

"You could just keep me. Why kill me and only keep a tiny bit of my magic when you can have the real thing?" Okay, now we were getting somewhere.

He threw his head back and laughed. "Oh, you're even more than I could've imagined. Love that sense of humour, gorgeous. Unfortunately, I can't keep you because it would be too much of a drain on my powers to keep you in line. You're a powerful witch, and I don't want to sleep with one eye open forever."

My befuddled brain thought it would be a good idea to stroke his cheek. My thumb ran along his lip. "Maybe we'd be good together? I don't mind sharing my power. I don't need all of it." I tilted my face up and kissed him. I hoped my subconscious had a brilliant plan because this wasn't looking good. At this rate, I'd be bedded then dead in no time.

He groaned and pulled back. "Hmm, you're more

dangerous than I thought." Was that worry in his eyes? But I hadn't done anything. Normally, I would've been calling lightning down by now, and that wasn't happening. I liked him. Killing him would make me sad. Somewhere deep in my brain, frustration pulsed, but it was puny, like a two-year-old trying to pitch a softball—a disappointingly short arc followed by a dazzlingly quick journey to the ground where it lay as evidence of my patheticness to mount any kind of offense.

Abruptly, he put his mouth to my neck and sucked. It kind of tickled, but then it hurt. Heat built in my stomach, and pressure on my insides made it feel like something large inside me was trying to crawl out via my veins. "What are you doing? I don't like that." I knew I should be freaking out, but I was in a loved-up haze.

He stopped and looked at me, his eyes burning with energy. Was that my magic giving him that glow? "Sorry, goddess. I mustn't forget that I want this to last."

I yawned, and my legs wanted to give way. I gazed at the bed longingly. "Can I maybe have a nap?"

"Of course. I'll just sit and watch."

That was one of the weirdest statements ever, but I was beyond caring. Sleep tugged at me—a need greater than anything else. He helped me to the bed, and I lay on top of the covers. Sooooo soft. My voice came out as a kind of drunken slur. "Oh, my shhooes. Ssssorry." Too tired to take them off, even though that would've been the polite thing to do, I shut my eyes and gave in.

Lily. Lily, can you hear me? Will's voice whispered in my head. Was I dreaming, or had the whole evening been a dream? Was it morning at home? I opened my eyes to pitch black. There was a body in front of me.

"Will?" I whispered.

There was no answer. I reached out and felt whoever it was. A bare arm, fairly muscular, but not Will. Will's arm was bigger, wasn't it? A hand clamped over mine, and it all came back. Crap. "Are you awake, gorgeous?" Tommy's sleepy voice confirmed the worst-case scenario.

"Mmm, kind of. I'm so tired though." Because I didn't know what else to do, and I didn't want him turning around, I buried my arm between his arm and his side and cuddled up to his back. I knew I should be scared, but I wasn't. I could happily lie here with Tommy forever.

No, Lily. I love you.

I swallowed and shut my eyes, willing my heart to beat slower. I fought the desire to do nothing, to give Tommy every-thing, and checked that my mind shield was up. Oh, wow, it'd survived so far. Even though he couldn't read all my thoughts, he could still have me do whatever he wanted. It was a bad thing, but he made it seem not bad at all. Those other women never stood a chance.

Lily, are you all right? Where are you?

In bed.

His anger briefly washed through me. *That's not what I meant. Do you know what address you're at?*

Nope. And I didn't care. I was here with Tommy, where I was meant to be. Wasn't I?

A tiny flame sputtered to life somewhere—in my heart?—

telling me this wasn't where I was supposed to be, that maybe Will was the person I loved. Hmm. I considered it. Remembering Will giving me a hug just yesterday, the safety and warmth of being in his arms, the emotion that swelled inside my chest every time he looked at me with that intense grey-blue gaze gave that flame strength, and it grew brighter, warmer.

That's it, Lily. I love you. You love me. Try and remember. The desperation and hope in his voice washed over me.

"Lily, time to get up." Tommy rolled over. "Open your eyes." I didn't want to, but I did, helpless to do anything but what the vampire witch asked. "Good morning, gorgeous." His magic tingled my scalp, and the lights turned on.

Sleepy, I smiled at the love in his eyes. "Good morning." Hmm. He looked even more handsome than yesterday. *That's his talent talking, Lily. Don't fall for it.* I started, Will's voice in my head totally unexpected.

Tommy's brows drew down. "What's wrong?"

"Nothing. Just a crick in my neck. I'm not used to sleeping with this pillow." I gave him an "I'll be okay" smile. It was nice to know that even if I was losing the battle of wills, my subconscious was doing its best.

"Sorry, darling. Let me give you a neck massage." I turned my back to him, and he kneaded my neck and shoulders.

"Mmmmm, that's good." But then his mouth was on my neck, sucking. A small pit of fear opened in my belly, along with the portal to the river of magic. He was feeding again. Waves of euphoria pulsed through me. But there was something else I recognised this time. The wrongness of it.

That's right, Lily. Fight it. Please fight it.

Tears burnt my throat and sprung to my eyes. The anguish in Will's mind voice broke my heart. My poor Will. *Sweetie, I love you. I'm sorry.*

Don't be sorry, dammit! Fight this, Lily. You're one of the strongest witches ever. You can stop this guy. He's a vampire witch, remember? You need to stop him. He's killed other women. Fight, my Aussie witch. Don't give up. I can't live without you, neither can James and Millicent. And Imani will never forgive herself. He overheard her talking to you on the phone. Then he snapped handcuffs on her and magicked her unconscious. She blames herself for this. Your parents need justice. It can't happen without you.

Every word breathed life on the flame, and it grew.

But as Tommy fed, my will diminished. My veins burned. I closed my eyes, the energy needed to keep them open dissipating like morning dew on a hot summer's day.

The steel fingers of a cramp squeezed my stomach. I moaned and hugged my middle. The sucking stopped, the burning in my veins cooling to hot, then warm. Tommy pushed away from me. His legs swished across the sheets before he swung his legs over the other side of the bed and sat up. He spoke through laboured breathing. "Don't want to kill you yet. Your power is intoxicating. Better than anything I could've imagined. There's so much... so much." He must have turned his body because his palm landed on my hip. "A man could drown in your power." Sadness crept into his voice. "I won't be able to stop next time, I'm afraid. I don't know what I'll do without you, Lily. I'm sure I'll never experience anything as good as you ever again." He sighed.

"Can I use your bathroom?" Okay, even in my head that was weird. He was casually talking about killing me, and all I could think about was my need to use the toilet. Where were my priorities?

"Let me show you." He jumped up and stumbled.

"Are you okay?"

He placed his palm on the wall for balance and ran a hand through his sexy bed hair. His boyish grin gave me butterflies. I knew I should hate myself right now, but reality was a distant island in the fog—I knew it was there, but out of sight, out of mind. After a few moments, he took his hand off the wall. "I've never taken in so much magic before. It's a bit like being drunk. I can't work out why you don't use your power to get further in the world—buy some diamonds, a mansion, rule over the rest, you know."

I shrugged. "Those things aren't important." I smiled. "I'm happy. I have everything I need, except for my parents, but that's another story. Taking over the world would be so much hard work. No thanks. Now, where's your bathroom?"

He was a bit wobbly on his legs—and so was I for that matter—but he took me out and to the next door down the hall. Thankfully, he left me alone to do my business. When I was done, I washed my hands and caught my reflection in the mirror above the vanity. Gee, I was pale, and those dark circles under my eyes hadn't been there yesterday. I blinked, tears coming unbidden. I was going to die here with so much left undone. Would they still raid the warehouse tomorrow…? Oh my God, that was tonight!

I stared into my own eyes and begged myself to wake up and try harder. That I was even having these thoughts gave me heart. If I could keep my distance from Tommy, I'd have a chance. Then an idea formed. But I'd need time to rebuild my strength. If Tommy decided to feed again in the next hour, I didn't know if I could do it. I had to stall as much as possible. Fear slithered in my belly.

Atta girl. I jumped, Will surprising me again. *Can you look out a window, see if you can tell us of any landmarks? Or even turn your phone on so we can track it.*

I can try. Being in a different room to Tommy helped clear my head, but as soon as I was back in front of him, the fog would return. Anger worked its way up my throat, and I gave a low growl. *Will, every now and then, remind me of the plan. Just say "the plan." Okay?*

Okay.

The door opened, and Tommy stood there, eyes narrowed, his attractiveness hitting me full force. The brain fog returned. "What are you doing in here? You flushed the toilet ages ago."

I shrugged. "As you can see, nothing. Just looking at myself in the mirror." I grinned and went to him, sliding my arms around his middle. I rested my head against his naked chest.

His arms came around me. "That's better now, isn't it?"

"Mmmhmm." I tried to sink back into myself, find that flame of defiance I'd need to survive, the plan I needed to implement. If I could focus on that long enough, I'd get out of this. If his talent smothered me again, well....

Tommy turned me around. "Time to go back to bed."

My stomach grumbled, trusty old thing that it was. "I'm hungry. Can I have something to eat?"

"Hmm." As he considered, it growled louder. "I suppose everyone's given a last meal, aren't they? What do you feel like?"

"Since it's my last meal ever, can I have a few minutes to

decide?" Deep down, in the pitch darkness of my innermost thoughts, terror at the immediacy of my demise issued forth, but Tommy's barrier was too strong, and only a squeak reached me. I knew I should be more worried, but I just couldn't be.

He leaned down and kissed me passionately without taking any power—something to be thankful for. "You're my favourite. Did you know that? I can certainly give you a few minutes; then maybe we can spend some time *together*." His gaze darkened with lust. "After that, unfortunately, it will be time to say goodbye."

I looked up at him with puppy-dog eyes. "Do you have to kill me?"

Regret contorted his face, but that was as far as it affected him. "I'm afraid so. I don't like getting attached. Plus, there's the sweetest moment when I take everything you can give. That last drop is always the most satisfying, when I'm holding so much that I think I'll burst. It's the most incredible sensation in the world."

Sickeningly, I was happy for him. "Lucky you. Don't you feel guilty about killing people? Couldn't you just drain power and move on?"

"That wouldn't be as much fun. Trust me, the power of the last drop makes me feel like the king of the world. Taking power on death is the most beneficial too. I not only take the magic from the river, but I get the last of a witch's essence. It's at that point all your talents shift to me." His beatific smile held me captive. There wasn't a stronger talent I'd come across. With everyone else, their talents were useful, but they weren't their life. It seemed that his talent made him who he was—a vampire witch. I wasn't photographer witch, and James wasn't honesty witch. Tommy's talent wasn't a means to an end—it was the end.... *He* was the end.

If I couldn't get my crap together and hold fast against his will, thousands more would die.

Will, if you're there, don't leave me, please. I need you so much right now.

His presence filled my mind—warm, kind, strong, and stable. *I will never leave you, Lily.* Beneath the suffocating layers of desire for Tommy, that flame of reality and love shone small but bright. My love for Will and my family would give it enough oxygen to survive... or so I hoped.

It was the last coherent thought I had for a while.

Tommy grinned, his magic enveloping me in a web of contentment and happiness. "So, what are you hungry for?"

It was time to choose my last meal, and then it was my turn to be dessert.

❧

I managed to stretch my meal out to an hour. I'd never chewed so slowly in my life. Even though I ate in a haze of Tommy-induced bliss, my survival instinct was strong. Will reminded me twice about the plan, but it wasn't time yet. There was something else I needed to do, but I couldn't remember. I knocked my forehead with my knuckles a few times.

Lines appeared in Tommy's forehead. "What are you doing?"

"I can't think straight. It's annoying."

He smiled smugly. "Yes. Sorry about that. You know, you

worried me when we first met. You didn't fall all over me as I'd hoped. You held out longer than all the others."

"How many others have there been?"

He scratched behind his ear, thinking. "Hmm, let's see." He nodded his head rhythmically, maybe counting. "I'd say close to three-thousand, give or take."

My mouth dropped open. It seemed I could still be shocked about something. "How old are you?"

He grinned. "It's not polite to ask a man's age. How old do I look?"

"My age. About twenty-four."

He laughed. "I'm one hundred and four." I blinked and stared. How was that even possible? He laughed again. "I know, right?" I'd kissed him. I knew that should be gross, but it didn't affect me, at least not on the surface.

It is gross, Lily. Trust me. Will's tone was dry.

Can you hear all my thoughts?

Yes.

Why can't I hear yours?

I have no idea.

Hmm, that didn't seem fair. But what did it matter? I was going to die soon. *Can you say goodbye to everyone for me? I've just had my last meal.*

His voice took on a panicked tone. *I thought you said you had a plan?*

Oh, I do, but it might not work. You know how it is.

He swore.

"Lily, hello? Earth to Lily." Tommy leaned forward in his chair, his hands on my shoulders.

I blinked as if waking up. "Oh, sorry. Just in my own head. I go off with the fairies a lot." I smiled.

"I noticed when I brought you here. You made it so easy for me to make that doorway. Anyway, enough chitter-chat. You've had your meal, and now I want mine." His predatory grin elicited a squeak of fear from deep down inside me. I swallowed as he stood and pulled me up with him. He turned me around to face the door, which led to the hallway and his bedroom. "Let's go."

As we walked, his magic tickled my scalp—was he strengthening the mind numbing? I shuddered with cold. It was as if something warm and anchoring had just been removed from my body. Could someone really steal your heart? Because that's what it felt like.

When we reached his bedroom, he grabbed my upper arm. He put his mouth to my ear and hissed. "You've been talking to someone, haven't you?"

Adrenaline shot through me. "Um, when?" I wanted to say no, but it wouldn't come out. That was the best I could do.

"Just before. Someone's figured out how to communicate with you. Well, I've put a stop to it. You can't keep anything from me." He shoved me, and I landed bum first on the bed. "Now wait here. I'll be back in two shakes."

As soon as he walked out, the suffocating vibes lessened, and I could think a bit more clearly. *Will. Will, are you there?*

No answer.

So it was true. He'd cut off my communication. I took a deep, shuddering breath. Now what? I stared at the door, my heart racing. The more his power wore off, the more terrified I became. What was I supposed to remember? *Come on, Lily, think, dammit.* I jumped up and ran to his wardrobe. Crossing the fingers on one hand, I opened the door with the other. Yes! My coat was there. I went through my pockets and grabbed my phone. Damn, it was off. I tried turning it on, but it was out of charge. Just before I shut the cupboard door, I noticed the wide-brimmed hat. That must be the one he'd been wearing in all those photos I'd taken. There was nothing I could about that now, so I gave the room a quick scan for a charger. Nothing.

Tommy's footsteps came along the hallway, my happy feelings towards him growing as he neared. Before he suffocated me again, I remembered my plan. I had to keep repeating it so I wouldn't forget. I shoved my phone in my bra just before he entered the room.

The plan. The plan.

Before I lost too much of my wits, I ran to him and threw my arms around him. Putting my hand on the back of his head, I pulled him to me, giving him a passionate kiss. If we were doing this, it was going to be on my terms.

"Mmmm." His voice vibrated against my lips. He stopped kissing me and put his mouth to my neck.

This was it.

I tried to disassociate myself with what was happening, sink what awareness I had beneath the strata of pleasure and fog. *The plan. The plan.*

My timing had to be perfect. Too early, and he wouldn't be far gone enough, too late, and I wouldn't have the energy for it.

His will kept tugging, desperate to pull my feelings back to the present, but I burrowed deeper, shut my eyes against the building fire in my veins and focussed on the portal where he gradually drew more and more magic from the river.

Before I enacted my plan, I diverted some magic to my phone. *Charge it*, I begged the universe. I hoped it heard me.

Tommy sucked harder, sending a spear of pain through my neck. Sweat dampened my skin, and I panted. It was as if someone had just turned the thermostat to sixty Celsius.

Tiredness swept over me, and I knew this was it. Now or never.

He groaned.

It was go time.

I sucked in a deep breath and concentrated on the golden river pouring through me. I willed more to come. Faster and faster. The cascade roared, eliminating all other sounds. The golden magic became rapids scouring through me, burning everything else away. I hadn't felt anything, but I knew we'd fallen to the ground.

With weak hands, I held onto Tommy's burning skin. He tried to pull away, but I syphoned more and more and gripped harder. I'd kill myself if that's what it took—I was dead anyway—but he was coming with me.

I forced the searing magic into him, my palms scorching. He screamed.

"Have it all!" I croaked, my voice raw.

"No!" He'd stopped sucking, but now I was pushing it into him, unrelenting. He'd wanted the most powerful witch in Westerham—well, he'd got her.

"Enjoy dessert. It's the last one you'll ever have." My hoarse voice came out as a whisper.

With the last of everything I had, I tried to drain the river.

I gritted my teeth against the pain of a thousand knives lancing my insides, my skin, and released everything with a final grunt.

The power slammed into him, wrenching him from my arms. The thud as he hit the wall was the last thing I heard as the river of power drowned my consciousness in its deadly rapids.

I was done.

CHAPTER 11

Gentle rocking. Low voices. Vibration against the ground.

Where was I? Had I somehow made it onto a boat?

"Lily, please wake up." A familiar voice, one that made joy blossom in my chest.

It wasn't easy, but I managed to open my eyes. Will knelt on the ground, cradling me in his arms. I smiled, happiness returning to the places Tommy had stolen it from. "Hey, you." My raspy voice sounded like I'd just smoked ten packs of ciggies. I coughed, and my stomach spasmed in pain. "Argh." As incredible as it was to see Will's face, I shut my eyes. The pain and exhaustion were too much.

But I'd survived.

"Beren," Will said. "She's awake."

A rustle of clothes as someone knelt next to us. Beren's tone was gentle, encouraging. "Lily, can you open your eyes?" I did as asked. Beren smiled. "Okay, I'm just going to put hands on you and see where you're at. I won't do anything else. You might be too weak to take a healing."

Imani came up behind Beren and looked down at me, her eyes steeped in worry and guilt. "I'm so sorry, love." Her forehead scrunched, and her eyes glistened. This was the closest I'd ever seen Imani to crying.

"It's not your fault." I gave her the biggest smile I was capable of. "He was always after me. He would've found a way." I shut my eyes briefly, then opened them. "Did you guys get here just in time? I finally managed to turn my phone on." I knew they'd wanted to track me, but if I'd used my magic before Tommy was draining me, he would've noticed and shut me down.

Will's expression was full of love and pride, but something else simmered just below the surface. "We got here too late, my love. It was all over. I'm sorry. We failed, but you did just fine." Ah, so that's what it was. They thought they'd failed—but they hadn't. They were here now.

My heart, as tired as it was, raced. I sucked in a breath. "Where is he? Did he get away?"

Imani smiled, her eyes turning to granite. "You killed him. Well done, Lily. How did you do it?"

"I think that's enough for now." Beren looked at me.

I shook my head. "Where is he? I need to see."

Everyone turned their heads to look at the far wall. Will helped me sit up and turned so I could see. Tommy's half-naked body lay broken on the floor, the plaster wall cracked. Blood had trickled down his face, and his arm and stomach were blistered and black. His arm must've been where I'd held onto him, and his stomach, well, that was the centre of his magic. I looked at my palms. They were red, but not too bad. After all the strong emotions he'd pushed onto me, the only thing I felt now was relief. He would never hurt another witch. I looked at my friends. "You guys didn't fail. You're here now, when I need you the most. He took my will, but underneath it all, my love for you guys kept me going."

Will squeezed me tighter. Beren cleared his throat. "Sorry to be the party pooper, but it's time to see how you fared." He placed his hands on either side of my head. His magic tingled my scalp as gentle warmth soothed my insides. After a minute, he stopped and sat back. "Everything's kind of a mess, and I don't think you have enough left for me to heal you. A good night's sleep should help, and tomorrow morning, I'll come by."

That didn't sound great. "What do you mean by a mess?" He pressed his lips together. "I can take it, B. The worst is over."

He sighed out his reluctance. "Okay. Everything has been scarred inside. It looks like a riverbank after a flood's passed through. It's blackened and rough, caught up with debris for want of a better description. You won't be magicking for a while. Sorry."

"It's fine. I don't care. I'm alive, right?"

He grinned. "Yep. You're alive." He, Will, and Imani looked at each other and shared the smiles.

"Can you get my coat out of the cupboard?" There was no way I was leaving my gorgeous red coat behind.

"I'll grab it." As soon as Imani had secured my coat, she looked down at Will. "I'll get the rest of the team here to catalogue this and remove the body. I'm sure Alena's father will be happy to get the good news that his daughter's killer's dead. In the meantime, I think you should get our girl home and in bed."

I secured my arms around Will's neck, and he stood slowly. "Okay, missy, let's get you home." He placed a tender kiss on my forehead. "You really need to stop scaring me like this."

"Sorry. I'll be more considerate next time." I gave him a tired smile.

He stared into my eyes, relief, love, devotion in his gaze. "You'd better be." His gaze turned serious. "We're postponing tonight's *dinner* to tomorrow night. There's no way I could focus on anything other than you right now." Warmth cascaded through me, and I nuzzled into his neck, breathing in the scent that was the man I loved. He was so much a keeper. He looked at Beren. "See you in the morning. I'll stay home till ten. Whether Chad likes that or not, I couldn't give a—"

"Yep, okay, mate." Beren laughed.

Will walked out into the hallway, made his doorway, and took me home… where I belonged.

CHAPTER 12

The next day, Beren came in the morning and healed me, but I was so drained, I slept the rest of the day. The new plan was for them to raid the warehouse that night, but even that wasn't enough to keep me awake and worrying. The only reason I'd woken up around 7:00 p.m. was because I'd begged Will not to go without saying goodbye. Plus, I needed to talk him into taking me to James's so I could watch the action on the monitors they'd set up for Millicent to watch. Imani and Will were going to be wearing body cams.

Will sat on the bed and kissed my forehead. "Hey, sleepy-head. How are you feeling?"

"A bit achy and totally exhausted, but no real pain. I was so tired, I didn't even have nightmares, but I'm sure they're coming." I sat up and adjusted my pillow so I could lean against it. "I need to tell you something."

His forehead wrinkled, and his voice was wary. "Go ahead."

"I wanted you to know that even though I kissed Tommy, I didn't want to. It was all his talent overwhelming me. I'm just so sorry." I blinked back tears because I could imagine how hurt Will was, knowing I'd thrown myself at someone else.

One of those tears escaped. Will wiped it off my cheek with a gentle finger. "Hey, I know. It's okay. I won't lie—it hurts, and it's going to take me a while to forget about it, but it wasn't your fault." He swallowed hard, his Adam's apple bobbing. "I need to ask you a question, and not for anything other than I'd like to know, plus tomorrow when you're interviewed about what happened, you'll have to tell them everything anyway. I'd prefer I heard anything relevant from you."

I had a feeling I knew what the question was, so I saved him the torture of asking it. "No, I didn't have sex with him. Kissing was all it was. He couldn't contain his desire to take my power long enough for anything else." I gave him a lopsided smile.

"Are you sure? You're not just trying to save my feelings?"

I shook my head and grabbed both his hands. "I wish none of this was painful for you, but I will always tell you the truth. Lying isn't my style. Kissing was it—not that that's great anyway."

He chuckled. "No, it's not, but… well… let's just say I'm relieved." He freed his hands from mine and wrapped his arms around me.

"Good. I love you, you know. You getting in my head was what kept me focussed. It was damned hard, let me tell you. I'm just glad he can't hurt anyone else."

"Alena's dad is satisfied we caught the guy. We found Lana's earring in his bedside table, and he had a bracelet of

Alena's, so at least it's confirmed. Chad hated congratulating us. It was rather funny, to be honest. Anyway, Alena's dad's asked to meet with you at headquarters tomorrow. I guess he wants to thank you. Chad's had to revoke your ban." He laughed. "You should've seen his face when that came out of his mouth."

I chuckled. "I can imagine. Moron."

Will checked his watch. "I have to go."

I was going to pretend like we'd already agreed I could go to my brother's. "Okay, just let me get dressed first."

He raised a brow. "No, you're staying here in bed, where you're safe and you can rest."

"Who said?" I raised my brow—two could play that game.

"Me and your brother. I don't want to go against orders. He's my superior."

I smiled. "And he's my brother. He's not the boss of me, you know. If you won't take me, I'll risk it and make my own doorway. I'm sure I've got enough strength back for that."

He pressed his lips together. After a moment of eyeballing me in a dismal effort to get me to change my mind, he threw his head back and stared at the ceiling. Once he was done having a meltdown, he looked at me. "Fine. Get dressed. But don't muck around. I have to get going." He smiled. "I do love you, though. I thought I'd lost you this time." His smile fell, and his gaze radiated fierce love. "I can't lose you, Lily. You're my person." He leaned towards me and kissed me. It was so much better than kissing Tommy. Love expanded in my chest until I thought I would burst.

When he pulled back, he had tears in his eyes. I stroked his face. "You can't get rid of me that easily, buddy. I'll be here to annoy you until one of us is dead… preferably when we're like a hundred or something."

"I'm holding you to that."

I held my hand out, and he shook it. "Deal."

I slid out of bed, dressed, and grabbed a coffee and toasted cheese-and-tomato sandwich to go. It probably wouldn't even hit the sides, but I could grab more food at James's later. Healing and magic took it out of a witch. Come to think of it, my jeans were looser than last time I'd worn them. Not that I needed it, but now I had a good excuse to fill up on double-chocolate muffins.

Will made a doorway, and I went through to James's reception room. I knocked. They had a video intercom, so Millicent knew it was us before she flung open the door. "Lily!" She threw her arms around me and squeezed.

"Hi," I said in a strangled garble.

She released me and laughed. "Sorry. It's just so good to see you… alive." Yep, that was my family, never sugar-coating anything.

"It's good to be alive, and it's nice that people care."

She linked her arm through mine and pulled me out of the room as Will entered. She threw a "Hi, Will" over her shoulder.

We were the last to arrive if the crowd in the living room was anything to go by. Imani, James, and Beren stood just inside the doorway chatting. As soon as they saw me, they lined up for a hug. Once all the happy greetings and enquiries as to my health were out of the way, plus a lecture from James about how I shouldn't be out and about, I sat on the couch—where Bagel and Cinnamon climbed my leg and sat in my lap

—and gazed at the TV screen that had appeared on one wall. It took up half of said wall. It was massive and divided into four pictures—two at the top and two underneath. "Wow."

Imani laughed. "Yeah, we didn't want Millicent to miss anything. It's all being recorded, and Millicent will have a mouthpiece so she can tell us if we need to get out of there ASAP. We'll all be wearing body cams." Which meant one screen for each person. Even though James and Beren would be dealing with the guards, it was good to have them double as lookouts.

James clapped once, and everyone else gathered around him. I was too tired to bother getting up, and since I was just a spectator and worrier—rather than warrior—I felt it was fine for me to sit.

James, Imani, Will, and Beren were all dressed head-to-toe in black. It was a shame that witches hadn't invented clothes of invisibility yet. I'd love that, sneaking around scaring people or eavesdropping. Maybe I should work on it.

James looked at his three agents in turn. "Okay, we've been over everything numerous times today. Now, let's make it happen. Dana's father is hiding something in that warehouse, and we're going to find out what it is. I have a feeling the answer will bring us one step closer to finding out what happened to my parents." He flicked his gaze to me. We shared a moment; then he faced his comrades again and flicked his hand. Small earpieces materialised in everyone's right ear, and I assumed the video cameras were now about their person.

Millicent put on a wireless black headset. "Talk to me, one at a time." They each whispered something, and she stuck her thumb up each time. "Great. Now let's test the cams." They each faced a different part of the room so it was clear which screen was which. Will was top right, Imani top left, Beren bottom right, and James bottom left. "Okay. Thanks. You're good to go."

"Right," said James. "The vans are in place with landing spots waiting. Everyone ready?" Everyone responded in the affirmative, and my heart raced, sending a lump of fear to my throat.

"Good luck." This time I did stand. I gave each of them a hug goodbye. I knew they'd do their best, but sometimes things went wrong. Gah, not the time to be thinking that. I stayed standing as they each made a doorway and stepped through, taking four pieces of my heart with them.

After they left, I settled back on the couch, and Millicent sat in a wheeled office chair. Will confirmed he'd taken out the cameras, so it was James and Beren's turn to kidnap the guards. I bit my fingernails as I stared at the massive screen. The rats had snuggled back into my lap, their warm little bodies giving me some comfort.

The vision from James's camera wasn't super clear because it was dark, and there wasn't a lot of lighting between where the vans were parked and the factory perimeter car park. They were going to have to step into the floodlights illuminating the path the guards took near the building.

James stopped at the edge of the darkness. A chain-link wire fence stood between him and the property. The view from

Beren's camera was slightly different, close but not the exact same spot. In the distance, two men stood chatting. At least they weren't infallible—not paying attention. But they were witches, and they likely didn't expect an attack from others of their ilk, and they no doubt thought non-witches an easy adversary. Although, surely Dana's father expected someone to come after him eventually, unless he was arrogant and assumed no one would work anything out. He'd already killed to keep his secret.

My brother was waiting for something before moving. After a few minutes, the guards stopped chatting. One walked one way along next to the factory wall and the other the opposite way.

James turned towards Beren, and Beren gave a nod. Imani and Will materialised out of the darkness with bolt cutters and made short work of the fence, creating a hole big enough for all of them to climb through. It was weird seeing Will cut it while watching it being cut from his perspective. All the while my jaw clenched as I anticipated their discovery.

Imani and Will waited near the fence while Beren and James sprinted to one guard each. My gaze flicked from one square to the next to the next. The rats scampered off my lap as I slid forward, hanging my bottom off the edge of the couch.

Coordinated like the professionals they were, they each tackled their guard at the same time and were quick to slap cuffs on them, rendering their magic useless. I sucked in a loud breath when the needles came out. I placed one hand over my mouth and watched them inject the guards with a drug to knock them out. Once that was done, they flung the men over their shoulders like sacks of potatoes and dashed for the hole in the fence. As they ran towards the hole, Will and Imani bolted towards the factory.

So far so good, but would their luck last? Was there something they'd missed? A hidden camera?

My pulse throbbed in my neck. This was too much excitement for two days, for God's sake. I'd need to sleep for a week after this.

Will and Imani reached the factory. Will magicked a battering-ram to himself and broke the side door down. Impressive. The battering-ram disappeared, and he and Imani drew their guns and rushed in. There shouldn't be anyone in there, but you never knew.

In the bottom half of the screen, Beren and James were almost at the vans where they could safely monitor their captives. I flicked my gaze back to Will and Imani.

They jogged through the factory, guns in front, stopping every now and then to turn a full circle and check their surroundings. It was dark, though, so I had no idea what they hoped to see. "Do they have night-vision goggles?" Millicent didn't answer. I mustn't have been loud enough to penetrate her earphones. I asked again, louder.

She answered without taking her gaze off the screen. "Yes." After a moment, she spoke into her microphone. "The boys have the guards secured in the vans. Imani and Will are inside. It's all clear." They must all be able to hear what she said. At least everyone was up to date quickly.

I wished I could hear what was going on. It was eerie watching the night-vision cameras do their thing with no sound. Bagel voiced a string of different squeaks. "I'm sorry, sweetie, but I have no idea what you just said." I sighed. Maybe she recognised something and was trying to tell me?

Will and Imani systematically went from room to room. I checked my phone. Five minutes had passed since they'd gone in. How long did they have? Was there a backup security system or alarm we knew nothing about? I knew Will had disabled everything he'd had to when the rats had gone in. Hopefully that was it.

I quickly looked at the lower screens—the two guards were still out of it. Millicent spoke again. "All clear in the warehouse. All clear in the vans. Will, you've been in there six minutes. Get to the trapdoor."

Imani and Will left the room they were in and traversed a hallway, passed through two more rooms, and stopped. Will held his thumb up to Millicent. Imani walked into view and crouched to examine the large door set into the concrete floor. She stood and said something to Will. After a bit of back and forth, Will pulled a small disc out of his pocket and knelt next to the door. He placed the disc in the lock. Once he'd done that, he and Imani ran into the adjoining room. A flash, then they were on the move again.

"Oh my God, he blew the lock!" I looked down at the rats sitting next to me who were the only ones listening. They looked up at me with their dark round eyes. What they actually thought about the explosion was a mystery. I sighed again.

Imani and Will both grabbed the edge of the doorway where chunks were missing and pulled it over, like opening a giant book. It revealed stairs. They took their guns out again and started down.

I held my breath. What was down there? Was it a trap?

Will must've said something to Millicent because she stood and stared at the top two squares on the screen. She twisted around to give me a worried look, then turned back.

I wanted to ask what was going on, but I didn't think she needed the interruption. I clamped my teeth together, and pain shot up the back of my head. Fatigue swept over me, and I shut my eyes for a moment. *Please let them be okay.* I could try sending Will a mind message, but that would take power I couldn't afford, plus if I surprised him at the wrong moment, I could potentially get him killed. Maybe this was karma—they would have felt just as helpless knowing Tommy had me somewhere secret and they couldn't help.

Imani's cam showed Will's back, but Will's cam showed—

My mouth dropped open, and I stood. "Oh. My. God." I walked slowly and stood next to Millicent, who turned to share a look of disbelief with me. We hoped to find something, but this…. What the hell was it?

As Will made his way through a huge basement area, his cam relayed images of people lying or sitting on the ground. A couple of them jumped up to stand and face the intruder. Thankfully, they were unarmed. So many people.

"What the hell did they just walk into?" I asked.

Millicent shook her head. "I have no idea, Lily."

Will stopped and magicked a light into being, illuminating everything. He faced one of the men who'd stood. He looked to be in his twenties, dark hair and beard, pale skin. His mouth moved—Will must have asked him a question. Millicent and I stayed riveted, staring in disbelief as things unfolded. Imani's screen showed her talking to a young man who hardly looked old enough to be legally able to work. What were they doing down there?

After a few minutes, Millicent pointed at her earphones to indicate someone was talking to her. I waited while she creased her forehead and nodded. She made mmhmm noises, indicating she was listening. "Okay. Yes. Of course." She turned to me. "This is too big for us, Lily. Those people down there work in the factory. They've been kidnapped and brought there from France and Bulgaria."

"Oh my God, they're victims of a people-smuggling ring! They're slaves?"

"You heard right." She looked away from me and put one hand over an earphone, listening again. She nodded. "Okay. I'll get the boys to transfer the guards to the PIB for questioning. We're calling this in." She pressed her lips together. "Yes, I know." She lowered her headphones and turned to me. "The game's up, Lily. We have to notify the PIB."

I blinked, adrenaline-fuelled nausea swirling up my throat. "You'll all get fired for this. Is there no way we can just return them to their homes and go after Dana's father ourselves?" I knew my suggestion was out there and probably stupid, but panic brought out the ridiculousness in me.

"No. This is… huge. We don't have a choice. Is this an isolated incident? Is this payback for families who Dana's father wants to punish? Are there more people involved, more places stolen people are being forced to work as slaves?" She shook her head. "There are too many of them for us to move somewhere else safely and too many questions. Where would we keep them? Like I said before—this is too big for us to handle. We need the PIB's support to stop it. We can't just leave them there and walk away either."

"But we went in illegally. None of this will stand up in court. Dana's father will sue."

Her poker face slid into place. "Well, we'll just have to come up with something now, won't we?"

I supposed we would.

CHAPTER 13

Soon after the crazy revelations, Millicent made a doorway for me, and I went home to bed. Everyone would be working well into the morning. They had to start interviews with each captive as well as the guards. Exhausted, I fell asleep straight away, sandwiched in between my fur babies. Nightmares plagued me, dark dreams in which I was locked in a basement with hundreds of other people, only brought out to toil inside the factory, then sent back to the underground. For those people last night, that nightmare was real.

Abby woke me at seven with a paw tap on my face, so I magicked food into her and Ted's bowls and fell back asleep. After that, I didn't wake up till mid-morning when Will was getting into bed.

I sat up and wiped the sleep from my eyes. "Hey, are you okay?"

He yawned. "Yeah, just exhausted. I have to go back there at seven tonight. I'm going to get a few hours shuteye."

"So you still have a job?"

"Today, yes. Chad hasn't had time to fire us. There's been too much going on."

"So, those people had all been kidnapped and forced to work for Dana's dad?"

"It looks that way. We have hours and hours of interviews to conduct, but everyone we've spoken to so far, that's their story. There's a lot to piece together. Anyway, we can talk about it later. I need sleep. How are you feeling?"

I checked in with myself. "Okay, actually. Still a bit tired, but I feel like I'm at 80 percent. Don't I have to go into the PIB today and talk to Alena's father?"

"Yes. Be there at twelve. Sorry I can't go with you."

"That's okay. I'll be fine. It's not like Chad can kick me out today." I smiled and gave him a quick kiss. "I'll let you get some sleep. I need to have a shower and eat. I'm starving."

He laughed. "I bet you are. It's hard to eat and sleep at the same time, and you've done a lot of sleeping the last couple of days."

"You know it." I climbed over him and hopped out of bed. "Night. Or is that morning?" I left him to sleep and got myself ready for the day. Soon enough, midday rolled around, and it was time to visit headquarters. Hopefully there wouldn't be any more vampire witches waiting for me, or Chad, for that matter.

When I arrived at the PIB, who should open the door but my favourite guard-cum-James's assistant. "Gus!" I gave him a huge hug. He awkwardly patted my back and stepped away. His cheeks were red. I laughed. "Sorry, Gus. I'm just so happy to see you."

He chuckled. "I get it, Miss Lily. I'm not much of a hugger is all."

I smiled. "Neither am I, usually, but I've had a crazy few days. Just appreciating anything normal right now. Are you still working as my brother's assistant?"

"Yes, but now Tommy's gone, I'm back here for a while until they find someone to replace him." He leaned closer to me and lowered his voice. "I heard what happened. I'm glad you're still here. Just thought you should know."

"Thanks, Gus. I'm glad I'm still here too. It was a close call. I seem to have had too many of those since I arrived in England. The closest I ever came to dying in Australia was when I almost trod on a red-bellied blacksnake on a bushwalk once. As soon as it felt me coming, it slithered away. So, it wasn't even that close."

He shuddered. "No thanks. I've heard there's lots of spiders, snakes, and jellyfish trying to kill you over there."

"Yes." I grinned. "Don't forget the drop bears."

His eyes widened. "The what?"

"The drop bears. Sharp claws, strong jaws. They're deadly. They drop on you from gum trees. We have to wear helmets when we're walking around anywhere there's trees."

He shook his head. "No thanks. I'll stay here, where it's safe."

I laughed. Hmm, safe my arse. I was pretty sure people had tried to kill me at least five times since I'd gotten here. I was going to run out of digits to count on soon. "Anyway, good seeing you. I have a meeting with a Mr Sorokina."

"You mean Mr Sorokin? Russian names are different for the man and the woman."

"Oh, okay. Mr Sorokin, then." That would've been embarrassing. "Thanks for the heads-up."

He smiled. "Any time. I'll take you there if you like."

"I'd like that very much, thanks."

He led me to the elevators, and we descended one floor. Once out, we went along the hallway to a door that looked like any other office door in the place. Gus knocked. A middle-aged woman with her blonde hair in a neat bun answered. Her immaculate appearance reminded me of Ma'am. Sadness nudged an unsympathetic elbow into my ribs, and I had to force a smile. "Hi. I'm here to see Mr Sorokin. I'm Lily Bianchi."

She smiled. "Hello, Lily. I'm Vanessa. Please come in." Okay, so I didn't know what Vanessa did around here, but it didn't matter. If she was an agent, she would have called herself Agent So and So. My natural sense of curiosity wasn't going to let this go. I'd totally be asking James later. She ushered me in. "See you later, Gus."

"Bye, Miss Lily. Good luck." Luck? Why did I need luck?

The office reception was just like James's and Will's— nothing special. Vanessa walked through the next door. I followed. Ribbons of invisible power skimmed my body, just like when I walked into Chad's office. Why did he have to be here?

My disappointment was short-lived, thank goodness. Chad

was nowhere to be seen, unless he was hiding under the mahogany desk, which wouldn't surprise me. Maybe after he heard what I did to Tommy, he was going to watch himself with me. I suppressed a chuckle.

"Ah, Miss Bianchi, thank you for joining us." The man who stood from the large chair behind the desk was dressed in a sky-blue shirt and tailored navy suit with gold cufflinks. His salt-and-pepper hair was long enough to be swept back in a neat but slick do. He shook my hand. "I'm Mr Moore. Lovely to meet you."

I only just stopped my mouth from falling open. This was the head director? I thought they were all supposed to have secret identities. I mean, just because I didn't know his real name didn't protect him. I knew what he looked like. Wasn't that more sensitive information? "Lovely to meet you to, sir."

"I'd like to introduce you to Maxim Sorokin, Alena's father."

I turned to the man standing to my left. He was about six-foot tall, black hair, maybe dyed, with blue eyes and a solid frame. He was dressed in more casual, but still expensive-looking, clothes, but it was his face that told the story. Dark circles under reddened eyes, a mouth reluctant to smile, arms hanging forlornly by his side as if he didn't know what he should do with himself. This was a broken man. "Miss Bianchi, I want to thank you for killing my daughter's murderer." His voice was steady, low, his accent a heavy yet cultured mixture of Russian sprinkled with British. Despite his grief, his voice didn't waver. I admired his strength, to come and see me when he was probably barely holding it together.

I bit my tongue to stop my own tears—sadness for this man and his family rushing over me. But he didn't need me to cry when he was standing strong. I willed myself to be in control. "It was my pleasure. I'm only sorry he came after me last."

He shook his head. "We cannot change the past, but you have brought my family and me a modicum of peace. My daughter would've been grateful to know that he can't hurt anyone else. She dedicated her life to justice."

"You must be very proud of her. I know she had a reputation around here of being a strong witch and one of their top agents. She was highly respected." I'd heard a few things, even though I'd never met her, and it didn't hurt to give him something positive he could hold onto.

This elicited an untightening of his expression but not quite a smile. "Thank you, Miss Bianchi. I also want you to know that if you ever need anything, anything at all, please let me know. My family owes you a great debt." I opened my mouth to argue, but he and the director both shook their heads. Mr Sorokin handed me a card. "Seriously, if I can ever help you or your family, please call me."

I took the card with no intention of ever asking for a favour. I hadn't saved his daughter, and in that way, we'd all failed. "Thank you." I put the card in my jeans pocket. "I appreciate you meeting me. And again, I'm so sorry we've lost Agent Sorokina."

A flicker of pain passed through his gaze. He cleared his throat. "Thank you." He paused and regarded me. "May I ask you a question?"

I gave a small smile. "Of course."

He took a deep breath and steadied himself. "Was it painful? Would my daughter have been in pain?"

I swallowed. What a question. "Not at first. And when it did hurt, it was stomach cramps and heat." Okay, so I downplayed it slightly—I didn't want him to know about the scalding veins and sensation of having the worst fever ever. He didn't need to know everything. It would've hurt, but I could concede that it wasn't the worse possible way to die.

"Thank you." He gave a nod and turned to Mr Moore.

He returned his friend's nod, then looked at me. "Thank you for coming down here today, Miss Bianchi. We're almost done, but I have one more question for you." He paused. It seemed it was the day for the hard questions. "What do you think of Agent DuPree Senior."

"Ma'am?"

"Yes."

I scrunched my brow. Why was he asking? I knew they were out to get her, and it was probably in my best interests not to say much, but stuff it. "She's excellent at her job, and I miss her. I don't know what's going on with her, but she's one of my favourite people. There's also no better person to be leading the agents at the PIB. She always knows what's going on and how to handle it." If he was looking for any information on her, he wasn't getting anything but praise. And if he was angling to find out where she was, I had no idea. Even if I did, as if I'd tell. At least he knew whose side I was on.

He nodded. "I see. Thank you." He turned to Vanessa. "When is my next meeting?"

She magicked a black diary to herself and looked inside. "In fifteen minutes. Plenty of time."

He smiled. "Good." He looked at me again. "Good day to you, Miss Bianchi. I'm sure we'll be seeing you again."

And with that, the heavy feeling of magic guarding the room disappeared. They each made a doorway and left. That was weird, leaving me in this room by myself. Righto, then. I was about to make my doorway and leave when the outer door opened. "Miss Lily, are you still there?"

I walked to the door in between rooms. "Hey, Gus. I was just about to leave."

"You're wanted in the conference room."

"Oh. Should I be worried?"

He shrugged. "I don't know. The order was given by Agent Williamson the Third, but Agent Bianchi is in the meeting too."

I sighed. "Okay." Today was turning into a doozy. Did Chad just want to assert his authority and kick me out again, or did he want to fire my brother in front of me? Whichever one it was, he was going to earn a chewing out. I could bet he'd never heard half the insults I was about to hit him with. By the time we'd reached the conference-room door, I was riled up.

Gus knocked and opened the door. "Miss Bianchi to see you, Sir." Gus must've got the nod because he stepped aside, let me through, and left, shutting the door behind him.

Everyone was here, well, except Ma'am. Chad stood at the head of the table, an exhausted-looking James, Millicent, and Will to his left, and Beren at the foot of the table. This must've been important if they'd dragged Will out of bed. Poor guy. I frowned.

Liv sat to Chad's right, and Beren and Imani to her right.

There were two places left. Would I be staying long enough to sit in one of them?

James smiled. "Hey, Lily. Take a seat." Apparently, I would be here long enough.

"Okay." I warily went to the seat next to Will and sat. If I could sum up the feeling in the room, it would be smug. Imani even wore a smirk. This should be interesting.

"Now you've joined us, we can get this meeting underway." Chad sat and folded his arms. His irritated expression was less than welcoming, and the worst was probably yet to come. But it was cool; I had my insults ready. "Lily, I'll start with you." He glared at me down the table. My stomach fluttered with nerves because I hated confrontation, but I was ready. "You're hereby allowed back on the premises. And in light of your killing of the vampire witch, I'm okay with you being contracted to aid in our investigations." His lips pressed together in a thin line. What had it cost him to say that? "Well, aren't you going to thank me?"

I lowered my chin and raised my brows, to stare at him with all the disdain I could muster. "No." He hadn't insulted me, so I couldn't insult him back, and considering he was saying I could come back if I wanted, well, I'd look silly for stirring things up, but it didn't mean I had to be nice to him.

He didn't quite know how to deal with my short, to-the-point answer. He did make sure not to look at my brother or Imani, who were both smiling. I, however, was still too cranky to smile about this. Let him squirm. My annoyed face would get the job done much better today. After a minute of indecision, he must've decided there was nothing left to say. He looked at the far end of the table, but not at Beren—his gaze was aimed at the wall above Beren's head. "Right, Agent Bianchi, you can tell the others what I've decided."

James smiled. "It would be my pleasure."

"I bet it would," Chad grumbled, still staring at the far wall. I looked across the table at Millicent, and we shared a smile. Had Mr Moore forced Chad to back down, and if so, why? Was it because we'd cracked a people-smuggling case or because I helped his friend by killing Tommy? And why such a huge about-face. Surely whatever agenda the directors had had before was still valid? Not to mention, the director had just shown up and revealed himself. I'd thought their identities were supposed to be top secret. Things just got curiouser and curiouser. Can't say I'd look a gift horse in the mouth though. Watching Chad have a toddler tanty was the highlight of my day.

"First of all, I'd like to welcome back my incredible sister, who singlehandedly took down a vampire witch." Everyone clapped—Chad didn't, but since I considered him a non-person, I wasn't counting him.

I blushed at the applause. When it died down, I smiled. "Thanks. I appreciate the applause, but it's not necessary. You guys put your lives on the line for others every single day. You deserve all the accolades too."

"It's our job, but thanks." My brother smiled. "Oh, a small piece of information, we found a few pieces of jewellery at Tommy's place, and one of them was a pendant owned by Jasmine Harris, the girl he followed home from the nightclub." At least her family had closure now.

I still had to know something. "Have they found her body?"

"No, I'm afraid. And I don't know that we ever will." James's statement gave me pause. Why hadn't I already asked him? I should've thought of it before now. Crap.

Imani put her hand up, and James gave her a nod. She looked at me. "I'm so sorry about what happened that night, love." She shook her head, sadness on her face. "He overheard our phone conversation about where I'd be meeting you, and when he slapped the cuffs on me, my magic disappeared. He elbowed me in the head and knocked me out. It wasn't till I woke up and crawled out of the room he'd shut me in that I managed to raise the alarm. It's all my fault."

I shook my head vehemently. "We've been through this, Imani. It's not your fault. He was waiting for me. If not then, he would've found another opportunity. He told me he'd come to Westerham just for me. I don't blame you at all. Promise me you'll forgive yourself. For me, there's nothing to forgive. You did nothing wrong." I stood and walked to her chair. Then I bent and gave her a hug. I squeezed hard, hoping to convey how much she meant to me. When I returned to my chair, James asked me another question.

"How did you kill him, Lily? With you being out of it afterwards and then everything else happening, I haven't had a chance to ask."

"A bit of luck and some determination. He left the room for a couple of minutes, and it was enough for the brain fog to clear. As soon as he came back, my brain immediately fogged, so I initiated things." I gave Will an apologetic look and grabbed his hand. "I'm sorry."

He gave me a sad smile. "It's not your fault, Lily. It's who he was. I'm sure he could've gotten any of us to kiss him if he'd wanted. He took away your free will."

"Thank you." My heart swelled with love. I was lucky to have him. "Anyway, as for the rest, well, he explained to me that after he gorges on power, at the moment the witch dies, he receives their talents. The first couple of times he fed off my power, it was like he was drunk, and he bragged how much he enjoyed it. I thought I'd help him have more, so once he was too far gone, and just before I lost all my energy, I force-fed him my power. His body couldn't cope." I shrugged. "And you saw the results. I figured if he wanted to eat, I was going to shove it in his gob and give him a meal to remember… or not, as the case may be." I grinned.

James laughed. "Yeah, I don't think he'll be remembering anything ever again." He shook his head slowly. "I'm awed at your power, Lily. I don't know if anyone has ever killed a vampire witch by themselves and without shoving anything into their belly."

"Maybe no one has ever had enough power, so they needed a boost?" As I spoke, Chad, lips pursed, stared at me like we were two four-year-olds and I had a toy he wanted but wouldn't give up. He had power as head of operations at the PIB, but how dangerous was he really? I'd have to watch him from now on. Now he knew I was strong enough to kill a vampire witch, was I more of a target? Or was he too stupid to care?

"Seems that way," said Beren. "We're just glad you're as strong as you are. You've done the whole world a favour."

I smiled. "It was my pleasure."

James laced his hands in front of himself on the desk. "Thanks, Lily. Now, our next order of business is Regula Pythonissam and their slave trade." My mouth fell open. We were really doing this, bringing it out into the open. Chad winced. Why, I couldn't fathom, but it was noted. James frowned at his boss—looked like it was doubly noted. "I've explained aspects of our investigation to Mr Moore, the head director." The director I'd met today. Was he our only supporter in this? At least the top guy had our back for the moment, which was better than nothing. "He's retroactively authorised all the steps we've taken. Due to the dangerous nature of RP, our actions will stand up in court. We don't have to operate under laws that restrain the police, especially in matters like these where many lives are at stake." He looked at everyone in turn. "As a consequence, no one will be losing their jobs." Relief slammed through me, and everyone smiled, well, everyone except you-know-who. He pouted. At least it was entertaining watching him suffer. I wanted to ask about Ma'am, but I decided that since she wasn't here, that spoke volumes. Maybe getting her back was asking a bit much at this point. At least it looked like we had full PIB support in our efforts against RP. That would make so much difference… as long as Chad stayed out of our way.

James unlaced his hands and stood. "Okay, crew, I can see how exhausted you all are. You're dismissed until tomorrow morning. Go home and rest. See you all later. And thanks for breaking this case wide open."

We all stood and gave each other goodbye hugs. It'd been an emotional and trying few days. At least they were all leaving here with jobs, and the target was off my back for now. The fact that Chad wasn't happy about it was a problem for another day.

Will made a doorway for both of us, and we happily went home. As good as that was, there was a small emptiness inside me. Something, or someone, was still missing. I had to wonder where Angelica was and if we would ever see her again.

CHAPTER 14

Five days had passed since the PIB meeting where everyone had managed to keep their jobs. Since then, they'd all been working like crazy, trying to sift through all the information and interviews. Yet again, Regula Pythonissam had made life hard for everyone. So, here I was, on a Monday, sitting at the kitchen table missing Will and drinking my cappuccino while Abby and Ted ate their breakfast. Everyone had worked the whole weekend, so I was totally over being by myself, at least without other human company.

I magicked my phone to myself. Ooh, two messages! They were from my friends in Australia. I scrolled to the first message and read. My mouth fell open. Oh my God. How did I not realise what date it was? April 29. I supposed a lot had been going on, and I'd pretty much slept my way through the last few days, although I was feeling back to my old self now, or was that older self?

Hey, Lily girl. I hope you have a fabbo birthday. Miss you, gorgeous.

Have a vino for me, sweetie. Michelle xx. She'd attached a cute meme of a squirrel holding a birthday cake with one candle on the top. It said, "Happy birthday to my favourite nut." I laughed, then sighed. I missed my girlfriends. The other message was from my other best friend. At least they hadn't forgotten, although I couldn't be too hard on Will and my brother. They had so much going on, and if I were honest, I'd forgotten my own damned birthday because I had no idea what day it was. Everything blended together when you spent most of your time at home. And as far as Imani and Liv were concerned, I wasn't sure I'd ever told them when my birthday was, or if I had, it was in passing, and it's not like they would have written it down.

I'd just call Will later and ask him to grab me a double-chocolate muffin on the way home. I could celebrate with that. Mmmm, chocolate. As I swallowed the last sip of coffee, I marvelled that I'd been here for a year tomorrow.

So, it was my birthday, and almost my first anniversary of being in the UK. I shook my head. So much had happened. Crazy things. Things I could never have imagined 366 days ago. Hmm, life was weird. How would things have panned out if my parents had never disappeared? Would James have stayed in Australia, or would my mother have sent him to be an agent anyway? Would I have ended up here just the same?

And then the pain hit, as it did every birthday. I couldn't say the ache was less than last year. Tears burned my eyes, and I didn't hold them in. I did enough of that, but it was my birthday, and I'd cry if I wanted to, as that old song went. I let the tears fall—wet, warm drops dragging down my face, washing away a bit of birthday joy as they fell. I wanted my parents here to give me a hug, to sing me "Happy Birthday," to enjoy a piece of cake and a laugh. God, I missed them.

Abby finished her breakfast and came to me. She jumped on my lap and put her paws on my shoulder so she could nuzzle my cheek. I put my arms around her and gave her a squishy cuddle. Her warm softness and love seeped into me, and the tears stopped. "Thank you, cutie pie. I love you."

She purred. I was going to take that as an "I love you too." Ted came and stood next to my chair, but his attention was out in the hallway. He barked.

I jumped up and created a return to sender. A knock sounded on the reception-room door. At least it wasn't a sneak attack. "It's okay, Teddy. It's probably someone we know." I went and looked at the intercom screen and smiled. I opened the door. "Imani! What are you doing here? Is everything okay?"

"We need your help. It's just a small job. Because everyone's flat out dealing with the RP crisis, James sent me to ask if you had fifteen minutes to come take some photos."

"Ah, yeah, sure. But my secret is still secret, right?"

"Of course, love. He just wants a lead if we can get one. He'll figure out how to tie things together later."

I shrugged. "Sounds good. Where are we going?"

"That art gallery in Westerham. You know, the one your ex used to own." She laughed.

I rolled my eyes. "He was not my boyfriend. He was a murderer. The whole thing was just sad, really." I magicked my suit on and my camera to myself. "Ready." It was probably lucky she'd shown up when she did, because I didn't want to spend my whole birthday moping. At least I was being useful right now. Maybe I could talk her into accompanying me to Costa to grab that muffin.

"Okay, love." She made a doorway for us both to use. It went to a large storage room that had a couple of unopened crates and a stack of pictures leaning against the wall. "Did we come straight to the gallery?"

"Yeah. One of the owners is a witch, the other is a non-witch who knows about us. It's all good."

"So, what am I taking pictures of? It's not going to be horrible, is it?"

She pressed her lips together. "Not too bad. Come on, and I'll show you." She opened the door to the gallery and walked out. I followed.

A chorus of voices screamed, "Surprise! Happy birthday, Lily!"

I jumped, and my hand flew to my mouth. Oh. My. God. For the second time that day, a lump lodged in my throat, and stinging warmth invaded my eyes.

The gallery was decorated with helium-balloon squirrel heads. I laughed. A long table had been set up in the middle of the room, and it was filled with food and drink. But the most exciting, fantabulous thing of all were the people standing around clapping and grinning.

James stood with Millicent, who held Annabelle. Will, Sarah, Lavender, Beren, Liv, and Millicent's parents watched, happiness radiating from all of them. I finally found my voice. "Um… hello?" I laughed. "Okay, wow, that was… unexpected." I looked at James, then Will. "I thought you guys'd forgotten. I mean, I even forgot."

James laughed. "You mean we didn't have to do all this?"

I grinned. "I wouldn't go that far. I got a couple of messages from Australia, reminding me." I looked at everyone in turn. "Thank you so much. I can't quite believe it. This means everything."

Imani smiled. "We all chipped in and got you a present."

On that cue, someone walked in from the next room, holding a giant photograph with a red bow around it. My mouth gaped. "The black panther picture! Oh my God, thank you. Thank you so much!" I'd had my eye on this beauty since seeing it months ago. It was hundreds of pounds, and I couldn't justify spending it on a want rather than a need. "Honestly, I love it. Thank you!" I gave Imani a huge hug. I went around to everyone, leaving Will for last. I gave him a massive smooch.

"Get a room!" James called out. Beren laughed.

"Well, go look at it." Will gave me a little nudge.

It was huge. I carefully took the picture from the person holding it and lowered it to rest on the ground so I could have a better look without dropping the precious artwork.

I sucked in a breath. The best present of all was behind the picture. "Angelica!" Before she had time to react—and by that, I meant run away and avoid all physical contact—I threw my arms around her, the picture between us stopping me from completely squashing her. Surprisingly, she didn't try and get away. She actually gave me an awkward hug in return.

"Happy birthday, Lily." She disentangled herself from my arms, but her eyes shone with… was that love? "I'm so sorry I haven't been here for you, but things are happening. I won't talk about that now, but I want you to know how proud I am of you. You've become quite the witch in the last twelve months, and I'm sure your parents would be proud if they could see you now." We both teared up at that. She was so full of surprises today. If I could never have imagined my life in the UK, imagining Angelica showing her emotional side was even more unlikely, but here we were.

"Thanks. You know that means more than I can put into words. I know you're sometimes unhappy with my choices, but you've been like a second mother or at least an aunt to me, and for that, I'm so grateful. I've been so worried about you. Whatever it took for you to be here today, thank you."

She smiled. "For you, anything, Lily. I know I'm hard on you sometimes, but it's necessary. I wish it wasn't, but…. Anyway, today is a day of celebration, so let's keep it light. I can't stay long, so why don't we get to it."

"Sounds good to me." I placed the gorgeous picture against the wall, linked my arm in hers, and we joined everyone else. Waiters appeared with trays of champagne. We all took one, and my brother tapped his glass with a spoon.

Tink, tink, tink. "Can I have everyone's attention?" We all turned to face James. "We're here to wish my awesome sister a happy birthday. As the oldest in the family, I feel it's my duty to say something." He paused and gave me a smile. "If Mum and Dad were here today, I know they would be so proud. I am. You've become an incredible young woman, and a powerful witch. All in all, I think I've done a pretty good job." We all laughed.

I couldn't resist chiming in. "I love the painting, but you could've gotten a proper comedian. Come on." I earned some laughter for my trouble.

James grinned. "But seriously, I'm sure I speak for

everyone when I say I'm in awe of who you are and the kindness you show. You're not an agent, yet you put yourself out there every time someone needs you. So, thank you, Lily. You've made a difference to a lot of lives. I'm so glad you're here with me. Happy birthday, and happy one-year-in-the-UK-versary."

"Hear, hear," everyone said.

Will cleared his throat. "Mind if I say a few words?"

"Go right ahead." James stepped back, and Will stepped forward.

Will gazed at me, love shining from his eyes. How had I managed to bag such a sexy yet ethical man? He always knew what to say to make me feel better, and he even laughed at my jokes. "So, Lily, do you remember the first time we met?"

I laughed. "Ha ha, yes, Agent Crankypants. I thought you were gorgeous but a bit of a, um, there's no polite way to say it, so I won't." James and Beren laughed.

Will grinned. "I thought you were gorgeous, too, but frustrating and irritating." He winked.

"Yeah, but to be fair, I'm only like that with you."

He chuckled. "Mmmhmm. Moving right along…. As your brother said, you've grown into a powerful witch and a strong, brave woman. I've only shared a year of your life, but it's been the best year of my life. I can't imagine being without you. The day we met, I knew you were the one for me." He handed his champagne to James, who had a knowing smile on his face, and knelt in front of me. His magic tingled my scalp, and a rose-gold ring with a solitaire diamond floated in front of me. Someone's shocked breath reached me, but I only had eyes for Will. I held my breath as he opened his mouth. "Lily Bianchi, witch of my dreams, will you marry me?"

Tears spilled over my lashes. I laugh-cried, my words stumbling out. "Yes, yes, yes! I love you so much." The ring floated to my finger and slid on. Will stood and gathered me in his arms. He twirled me around to cheers and more applause. When he was done spinning, hc placed me down and his arms came around me.

He lowered his head. Our lips met, the butterflies in my belly having a party of their own. Surrounded by everyone I loved, I kissed the man of my dreams. No matter what came, this day would forever be ours. The last 366 days had been the longest ever, but I'd do it all again if it led to this moment.

Will grabbed his drink off James—I still had mine, and I'd even managed not to spill it during all the marriage-proposal-and-spinning stuff.

James raised his glass. "To Lily and Will!"

A chorus of voices sung out. "To Lily and Will!"

Now that was a toast I could totally drink to.

ALSO BY DIONNE LISTER

Paranormal Investigation Bureau

Witchnapped in Westerham #1

Witch Swindled in Westerham #2

Witch Undercover in Westerham #3

Witchslapped in Westerham #4

Witch Silenced in Westerham #5

Killer Witch in Westerham #6

Witch Haunted in Westerham #7

Witch Oracle in Westerham #8

Witchbotched in Westerham #9

Witch Cursed in Westerham #10

Witch Heist in Westerham #11

Witch Burglar in Westerham #12

Witch War in Westerham #14

The Circle of Talia

(YA Epic Fantasy)

Shadows of the Realm

A Time of Darkness

Realm of Blood and Fire

The Rose of Nerine

(Epic Fantasy)

Tempering the Rose

ABOUT THE AUTHOR

USA Today bestselling author Dionne Lister is a Sydneysider with a degree in creative writing. Daydreaming has always been her passion, so writing was a natural progression from staring out the window in primary school, and being an author was a dream she held since childhood.

Unfortunately, writing was only a hobby while Dionne worked as a property valuer in Sydney, until her mid-thirties when she returned to study and completed her creative writing degree. Since then, she has indulged her passion for writing while raising two children with her husband. Her books have attracted praise from Apple Books and have reached #1 on Amazon and Apple Books charts worldwide, frequently occupying top 100 lists in fantasy and mystery. She's excited to add cozy mystery to the list of genres she writes. Magic and danger are always a heady combination.

.

Printed in Great Britain
by Amazon

74273928R00123